SPECIAL MESSAGE TO READERS

This book is published under the auspices of

THE ULVERSCROFT FOUNDATION

(registered charity No. 264873 UK)

Established in 1972 to provide funds for research, diagnosis and treatment of eye diseases. Examples of contributions made are: —

A new Children's Assessment Unit at Moorfield's Hospital, London.

•

Twin operating theatres at the Western Ophthalmic Hospital, London.

•

A Chair of Ophthalmology at the University of Leicester.

•

The establishment of a Royal Australian College of Ophthalmologists "Fellowship".

You can help further the work of the Foundation by making a donation or leaving a legacy. Every contribution, no matter how small, is received with gratitude. Please write for details to:

THE ULVERSCROFT FOUNDATION,
The Green, Bradgate Road, Anstey,
Leicester LE7 7FU, England.
Telephone: (0116) 236 4325

In Australia write to:
THE ULVERSCROFT FOUNDATION,
c/o The Royal Australian College of Ophthalmologists,
27, Commonwealth Street, Sydney,
N.S.W. 2010.

HOT MONEY CAPER

What starts as a straightforward case of rich man's wife being blackmailed by ex-lover quickly turns into a matter of life and, more probably, death for cynical private eye, Mark Preston. How much does the gorgeous Ellen Ralph really know? Is he being set up and is she telling him everything? The Police think he's in with the Syndicate. The Syndicate think he's in with the blackmailer. How can he win the game when he doesn't know the rules?

Books by Peter Chambers in the Linford Mystery Library:

THE DAY THE THAMES CAUGHT FIRE
SPEAK ILL OF THE DEAD
THEY CALL IT MURDER
THE DAY OF THE BIG DOLLAR
DOWN-BEAT KILL
THE DEADER THEY FALL
LADY, YOU'RE KILLING ME
MURDER IS ITS OWN REWARD
THE HIGHLY EXPLOSIVE CASE
FEMALE — HANDLE WITH CARE
THE LADY WHO NEVER WAS
ALWAYS TAKE THE BIG ONE
THE VANISHING HOLES MURDERS
THE MOVING PICTURE WRITES
BOMB SCARE — FLIGHT 147
NO PEACE FOR THE WICKED

PETER CHAMBERS

HOT MONEY CAPER

Complete and Unabridged

LINFORD
Leicester

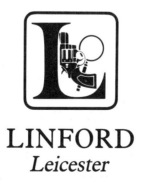

First published in Great Britain

First Linford Edition
published 1998

British Library CIP Data

Chambers, Peter, *1924–*
Hot money caper.—Large print ed.—
Linford mystery library
1. Detective and mystery stories
2. Large type books
I. Title
823.9′14 [F]

ISBN 0–7089–5263–1

Published by
F. A. Thorpe (Publishing) Ltd.
Anstey, Leicestershire

Set by Words & Graphics Ltd.
Anstey, Leicestershire
Printed and bound in Great Britain by
T. J. International Ltd., Padstow, Cornwall

This book is printed on acid-free paper

1

The sun was merciless that July.

It was now in the fourth week of total domination, burning away at everything in sight, animal, vegetable and mineral. I can't vouch for the vegetables and minerals, but the animals were getting near the end of their tether. The heat was everywhere, permeating, infiltrating, sapping away at people's vitality and patience. Especially patience. To top it all off, there had been two power failures, and when you have no power, you have no air-conditioning, so there was no respite indoors.

A guy in a bar told me he'd seen a cloud early one morning over Indian Point, but then, guys in bars will tell you anything. All I had to go by was the evidence of my own eyes, and it was their opinion there had been some celestial incompetence. What we were getting was the sun which should have been on duty over the Sahara Desert.

Monkton City sprawled moodily along the shoreline, sweating and grumbling, snappishly alert for slights or insults, and reacting immediately to samples presented. A misplaced cough or laugh was sufficient provocation for a fist in the mouth. Street assaults and domestic violence were up by around two hundred per cent, and the overworked police were stretched to the maximum and beyond. The criminal element, ever alert to opportunist situations, was having a ball. Stickups, break-ins and muggings were proliferating on a scale which was already well past the bounds of containment.

Newspapers and politicians were muttering about the breakdown of civilised society, the advent of a second Dark Ages and the like, which is usually a sign that somebody else wants a crack at the mayor's job.

Personally, I was bearing up to the conditions as best I could, by conducting a half-hearted search for a bond-jumper by name of Elias Schwarzkopf. Old Elias, a trusted employee . . . aren't they always — of the giant Houseproud domestic supplies chain, took the company payroll home for safekeeping and omitted to bring it back. He also removed one seventeen year old employee, Dolores Heffer, from the bosom of her loving family, presumably to help carry the money. What else would a fat sixty year old want with somebody's granddaughter? The indications were that these two had headed in my direction, so the least I could do was ask around. I could certainly use the ten grand reward, plus I wanted to see a man who'd admit to that name.

At the moment I'm talking about, I was sitting in the Paradise Grill, on the off-chance that Elias might come in to cool his wallet. I'd been there almost two hours, studying each arrival conscientiously, because I like to be thorough about these things. Later, I would move to the Hawaiian Bar for a similar stint, and maybe after that I'd cover Italian Eddie's, just to round out the day. That would add up to six hours of consecutive duty, which is more than most people could claim under those conditions.

A telephone bleeped discreetly below the bar counter. The jockey lifted a plastic Donald Duck and put the beak to his ear. Then he extended the thing in my direction.

"For you, Mr. Preston."

I didn't want my careful vigil to be interrupted.

"How do we know that?" I demanded. "Did you know there are thirty seven Prestons in the book, not to mention surrounding areas. It could be anybody."

"It could be, but it ain't," he returned sourly, "Look, this is getting heavy."

There was something in his tone suggesting if I didn't take it in my hand, he might wrap it round my ears. I took it.

"Well?" I growled.

"Mr. Preston, thank heaven I found you. My name is Ellen Ralph. Could you come out to my house right away? It's 2024 Boulder Drive."

I stared at Donald's beak, which was spouting all this unwanted information. The only Ralph I knew was a small-time pool hustler down on Conquest

Street, and he didn't have any wife named Ellen. He also didn't live on Boulder Drive, which is a long way from Conquest, geographically, financially and socially.

"I'm kind of busy, Mrs. Ralph," I hedged, making it sound like 'Miz', "Could you let me have some idea of what it is you want?"

"Not over the phone", she informed me, "But if you're here in fifteen minutes, I will pay you a cash bonus. One thousand dollars".

Even in the heat of the afternoon, there was suddenly a cool green feeling to the conversation. It wasn't the money, you understand. If a woman calls for help, it's every man's duty to respond. Besides, a thousand cash meant I needn't trouble Internal Revenue with the transaction.

"I'll be there," I promised, and handed Donald back to the bartender.

"Sounded like a nice lady," he offered, eyes agleam for some lascivious contradiction.

"I don't know any other kind," I assured him loftily, as I crawled reluctantly off the stool and headed for the door.

When I left the car, it had been shaded by the side of the building. Now, because I'd been so conscientious about waiting for Elias and his corrupted minor, the sun had sneaked around the corner and gone to work on the exposed metal. It was probably cooler inside than in that other place where the bad guys go, but I must have shed two pounds in the first mile. Boulder Drive is north of the town on the upper slopes, where the sea breeze gets a fair chance to work, and I was almost normal when I reached 2024. It was nothing special, for the neighbourhood. Two storeys of white stone, with a well-tended lawn and shrubbery front, sitting in about half an acre. There would be eight rooms, three bathrooms and a thirty foot pool in back, and you could pick up the whole thing for around one point four. Million, that is. Outside, there were three cars, a Cadillac, a Bentley, and a little Italian job capable of about four hundred miles per hour.

I walked up wide stone steps, enjoying

the quiet plashing of a fountain which stood to one side, and pressed at a bell which made a musical noise somewhere. Then I remembered to check my watch, anxious about the deadline. Thirteen minutes, I noted with satisfaction. I'd already earned one thousand dollars, clear of tax, a good start. I might not be doing as well as old Elias, but then I didn't have every badge in town looking for me either.

I heard the rapid click-clack of high heels in the distance, then the door opened and I got my first look at Ellen Ralph. Well, not exactly. I'd seen her before someplace, but couldn't recall quite where. She was very tall, five nine at least, with one of those graceful, athletic bodies so popular with fashion designers. Her hair was dark, and clipped short around the long oval of her face, skin stretched taut over high cheekbones, the kind of face which does not sag with the years. But it was her eyes which really held the attention. Enormous deep blue pools in the olive skin, pools filled with trouble as we inspected each other.

"Thank you for coming, Mr. Preston. Please follow me."

She'd had no need to ask. Men had been following this one without question, all her adult life, and I was not about to make an exception. It was cool in the house, what with the stone floors and high ceilings. She led the way into a large airy room, where french doors stood wide open at both ends. There was heavy Spanish furniture dotted around, but not so much as to make the place oppressive. In one corner were bookshelves, but the books were not part of the furnishings. They were all shapes and sizes, all manner of coverings, from tooled leather to tattered paper, and they were there because somebody read them.

She came to a halt in front of a white marble fireplace which hadn't seen a fire in fifty years. It could have been accidental that her head was entirely framed by an enormous gilt mirror. Slim tapering brown fingers fluttered at me.

"Won't you sit down?"

I nodded, and parked on the tapestry seat of an oak chair.

Despite her outward show of self-possession, the lady was in a state of high nervous tension, and the message had all been there, in the depths of her eyes. Even if she had been able to control her expression, there was still that thousand dollar bait to be explained. For that kind of money, I can contain my impatience, and I sat there looking hopefully enquiring.

Her quick red smile reached as far as her cheeks, but those eyes were untouched by it.

"Have you remembered yet?"

"Remembered?"

"Where you've seen me before," she supplemented.

"Oh." I wrinkled up my forehead. People like you to do that, it's a sign of deep thinking. "Well no, I can't quite . . . er . . . "

She nodded absently, as though the reply was as expected.

"It's that damn box," she explained mysteriously. "It eats up people like candy. I was top of the ratings, four straight series, now you can't even remember who I am. Or was", she added snappishly. "That Girl Susie. I'm Ellen Brady."

It came back to me then. The Susie show had been one of those runaway successes the money-men dream about. It had featured the exploits of a group of teenage kids in a Mid-West town, unknowns at the time, and Joe Public had loved it. I was talking to Susie herself, the harebrained leader of the pack. She was right about one thing. It couldn't have been more than three years since the series ended, and already I'd forgotten who she was. Now I had to say something to salve her ego.

"So you are," I grinned. "I can see it now. You'll have to forgive me Mrs. Ralph, but all this . . . ", and I waved a hand around to include not only the surroundings, but also herself, " . . . it's a long way from Main Street. Whatever happened to the show, anyway?"

"I happened to it, and one or two of the other kids. I was a twenty-seven year old teenager at the end. They decided to drop it while we were still ahead. I'd had enough anyway. I wanted more out of life than that. I married Joe Ralph, and here I am."

All very interesting, but it wasn't getting us any closer to the reason for my presence.

"I used to catch the show whenever I could," I said pleasantly, "But I keep some funny hours in my line of work. Can't always guarantee to stick to a time-table. Is your husband in show business?"

"Yes, he is," she confirmed, "Low profile. He doesn't get involved with studios or actors or that side of the business. Joe's a financier, one of the people who finds the money. They don't get their pictures in the trades, but they're the ones who matter."

I did some serious nodding, to let her know I had the picture. Off and on, over the years, I've had some brushes with that crazy half-world, and knew a little about how it worked. Also, I was trying to indicate that I now understood the set-up, not an unfamiliar one around those parts. Beautiful, successful actress marries oil-well and retires. All I didn't know was what I was doing there.

Ellen Ralph looked at her wrist, where a slim platinum bracelet must have held one of those eye-dropper size watches.

"Good heavens, it's past five o'clock. Joe will be home at six, so we don't have much time."

Then we oughtn't to be frittering it away on all this family history, I thought, but I merely waited.

"I'm being blackmailed, Mr. Preston."

The words came out low and fast, but not so fast that they escaped me. Blackmail had been near the top of my 'reasons for visit' list, and came as no surprise.

"What about, and how much do they want?" I queried.

"Twenty five thousand dollars", she replied.

Which was only half an answer, but I let it pass for the moment.

"Have you got it?"

To an outsider, the question might have seemed foolish. Given the house, the cars, my client's clothes and jewellery, twenty five grand might sound like spending money, but I've been around too long to make judgements on externals. I knew at least one multi-millionaire who allowed his wife one hundred dollars per month, and she had to account for every cent. Maybe the Ralph menage was that way.

"Yes, I have it", she replied, to my surprise. "I don't have it readily available, but I can get it. The trouble is, to raise that money without my husband finding out will take several days, even a week. This man says he won't wait that long."

I frowned.

"You mean you're prepared to pay?"

It wasn't what I'd expected. I thought she'd be wanting me to contact the blackmailer, lay some muscle on him and scare him off. If she was willing to meet the demand, why wouldn't he wait?

Her face contorted unpleasantly.

"Oh yes, I'll pay", she confirmed sourly. "I really don't have much choice about that. But I must have time, and that's where I'm hoping you'll be able to help me."

"You want me to see this man, explain

your position and persuade him to give you the extra days. Is that it?"

"That's it exactly. Will you do it?"

I made a face.

"I don't know", I admitted. "A lot depends on what he has, and what he's really after. Why should he take my word, when he won't take yours? And what's his big rush, anyway?"

"He says he has to get out of the country, and quickly. There are certain people looking for him, gangsters by the sound of it, and the money will be no use to him dead. So he says, at least."

That would explain his hurry but, if it were all true, he had nothing to gain by spilling the beans on my client. Nothing, that is, except possible revenge. Revenge for what?"

"Forgive my saying so, Mrs. Ralph, but this sounds kind of personal", I began gingerly. "What does he hope to gain by telling whatever it is he knows? He must hate you a lot if he's prepared to cause you a lot of grief at no profit to himself. I think you're going to have to tell me a little more."

She did some more of that arm-fluttering, then suddenly sat down, clasping her hands around excellent knees. The trouble with actors is, it's very hard to know when they're acting. I sometimes doubt whether they know themselves.

"I'm handling this badly," she confessed. "I should have told you from the beginning what this is all about."

I looked suitably grave then, and prepared myself to listen to some plausible, self-extenuating yarn. But I didn't know Ellen Ralph too well.

Not then.

"His name is Harry Mason, and he doesn't hate me at all. I met him in Palm Springs last winter. He's a dealer at a casino there, or was. Joe was away on business for a few days, so I took off, to break the monotony. I do that sometimes, and it's not usually too difficult to find a Harry Mason. I spent three days with him, then got back here before Joe returned from his trip. As you can judge, I'm not a very moral person, Mr. Preston. Do I shock you?"

I shook my head, slightly bemused.

"The only thing that shocks me lady, is your honesty. Mostly, when I hear these tales, they come wrapped in a thick layer of excuses. I appreciate your being so frank, it could save us a lot of mutual misunderstanding. I take it you never expected to hear from him again?"

"There was no need, that I could see. We both enjoyed ourselves, and that was to have been the end of it. He really isn't the blackmail type, though you may find that hard to believe. But he is desperate, and I'm his best source of revenue."

That was satisfactory as far as it went, but it still didn't explain why he would expose her, without profit.

"But if you can't pay in time, what would he gain by selling the story to a newspaper or whatever? They wouldn't pay anything like that sum, and in any case they'd spend days checking the story out before they printed it. The bad guys would still catch up with him."

She shook her head impatiently.

"That's not his intention. He says he'll go to my husband for the money. Joe would pay it, rather than have any public scandal, but it would be the end of the marriage. That is my dilemma, Mr. Preston. Harry's determined to have that money from someone, one way or the other. As he says, his life is on the line, and he can't play games."

"H'm."

I sat there a few moments, digesting what she'd told me. This was not one of those right and wrong situations, with room for a little negotiation this way and that. This was a question of time, and the man hasn't been born who can stop that old clock. If Ellen Ralph was to be believed, and I thought she was, there wasn't going to be much I could do to change things. But, and it was a big but, a lot depended on the extent to which lovable old Harry could be relied on.

"You obviously believe Mason's story about the trouble he's in. Did he give you any more details on that? I mean, what's he done that's so terrible the mob want to get rid of him?"

Her throat muscles tightened as she shrugged the brown shoulders.

"No, he didn't elaborate on that. I

know the kind of world he moves in, big-time gambling and so forth. It's a world where those things do happen, as you must know better than I."

"But you do believe him?" I pressed.

"Oh yes, I've no doubt it's true. After all, the details are hardly important, are they? Not to me. All I know is, I have until tomorrow morning to produce the money, or he'll go direct to my husband. Will you see him, talk to him? Please?"

She turned the whole works on me then, woman and actress both, and it was quite a blast. The air in that elegant room was suddenly electric with supplication, helplessness, half-promises and raw sex. A man would have to be ninety years old to resist an attack like that.

I got up.

"Where do I find Mason?"

As to what I intended to do when I saw him, I hadn't the least idea. All I knew was, I was standing there, buckling on this armour, and setting out to deal with the dragon, or whatever it was Guinevere happened to need doing at that moment.

Ellen Ralph had risen to her feet, the tip-tilted nose on a level with my chin, just about right for —

"He's rented a beach house down near Fisherman's Quay. He says he daren't risk a hotel, because that's the first place they'd look for him. He's rented in the name of Griffiths. I've written it down. Here."

She extended a piece of paper, and I struck it in my breastplate. There was just one more thing. My good luck charm.

"Er" I said, then paused.

"Oh, yes, I almost forgot." She held out a handful of bills. "One thousand dollars. You made it in fourteen minutes, Mr. Preston."

Thirteen, I amended mentally, but at these prices, who wants to quibble?

"Can I call you here, or will your husband overhear?"

She inclined her head.

"He's not an eavesdropper. I'll take the call in my bedroom. It'll be quite safe."

Now that we were fellow-conspirators, she seemed to have bucked up considerably, if those shining eyes were anything to judge by.

"Look, we have to be clear about one thing, Mrs. Ralph." I was heavy on the 'Mrs.' there, as much to remind myself as anyone else who might be listening. "I don't much like the sound of any of this, and if Mason's on the level about the danger he's in, I have serious doubts that I can shift him on this."

She put out one of those violinist's hands and drummed lightly on my chest.

"But you are going to try, and you're my only hope."

I mumbled something, and left her standing there. It's all very well for the Guineveres. All they have to do is wave a handkerchief, and get back inside the nice warm castle.

The rest of it is left to us dragon-hunters.

2

There had been a time in the development of Monkton City, where the harbour was the focal point. The natural bay, although small by comparison with its saintly rivals, Diego to the south and Francisco to the north, nevertheless affords deep-water anchorage close into shore. It had its part to play in the coastal trade, and even managed to corner a small percentage of the Pacific action. As a result, there was a healthy maritime connection, which lasted until a few years after World War II, after which it began its slow decline.

Alongside the ocean-goers, the great freight and passenger lines, there was also a fishing tradition, the little smacks buzzing in and out of the traffic like street urchins. This industry, too, had declined of late years, not because there weren't any fish to be caught, but because the independents couldn't compete against the refrigerated monsters which had moved into the trade. A few of the old-timers stuck it out, but there were no young men waiting to take their places, and the half-dozen or so survivors knew they were a dying breed.

Nowadays, the harbour area has something of the air of a ghost town, with its empty piers, idle warehouses, and cranes rusting where they stand. As I drove through it that early evening, there was only one cargo ship alongside, a creaking old tub flying a Panamanian flag, which can mean whatever you choose it to mean. Fisherman's Quay is a rather imposing title for a broken-planked wooden structure which juts out sixty feet into the ocean. To an untutored eye it seems to be in imminent danger of collapse, but then, it's looked that way for thirty years that I can swear to, so perhaps the untutored eye could do with some tutoring. With so many people having left the trade, there is a sprawling collection of deserted wooden shacks, which used to act as storehouses, spare part stores and so forth for the individual trawler-men. Some wily developer, realising the potential of these sites as vacation homes, had bought up half a dozen of them, refurbished, and given them a new lease of life as bungalows. They were ideal for the power-boat gang, the surfers and so forth, and had proved to be a highly succesful investment.

There was one drawback to the bungalows, but that was only known to local people, and newcomers had to learn the hard way. A dirt road ran along the rear of the buildings, so that the revellers could have easy access for their cars. Unfortunately, due to some seismic freak in an earlier millenium, there is a heavy deposit, along that section of the shoreline, of razor-edged flint-stones, and these seem to have a special attraction for rubber tyres. People who know the local topography find it prudent to leave their cars at the end of the quay, and make the rest of the trip on foot.

I pulled in, coming to a halt on some of the more reliable-looking planks, and found myself alongside a shiny new Toyota in bright blue. Somebody else evidently knew all about the flints, or had recently learned about them. Climbing out, I stood for a few moments surveying the scene. All the fishing boats were out, which meant they would be a couple of miles off-shore preparing for the evening catch. There was no other sign of life close to hand. Looking south, I could see the coloured sails of the small yachts at the pleasure end of the beach, where the pebble gave way to sand, and the real seamen were replaced by the yachting cap Bermuda shorts brigade. It was almost like the old world getting a sneak preview of the new, and finding it not much to its taste.

I pulled myself up sharply. There's something about closeness to the sea which tends to make me start philosophising in this unprofitable fashion. It's all phoney, anyway, because I don't have any such heritage in my background, nor even in my frustrated ambitions folder. As far as I'm concerned, all that salt pork and hardtack is strictly for the extras at Warner Brothers. I'll take a medium-rare steak any day in preference.

The address which Ellen Ralph had

given me indicated that Harry Mason was staying in the fourth beach house along from where I was standing. There was a bright red roof on it, and startling yellow wooden walls, and the owner had called the place Sea Dream. If all those reds and yellows started to occur in my dreams I should think it was time to visit the shrink, but luckilly I don't have too many dreams. Just nightmares.

A light breeze was coming in across the water in a forlorn attempt to offset the baking heat which had a day's start on it. The sun was on the decline by this time, but there was none of that 'dying rays' aspect one reads about. Instead, it seemed to be sinking in that same full glory it had enjoyed all month, full of malevolent promise that it would report again next morning, sharp and ready molten.

To wear a jacket in that heat would be to invite not only attention but suspicion, so I left it in the car, and set out in my shirtsleeves. That meant I couldn't pack any hardware, but I didn't see why Mason and I would get to the need for talking with guns. After all,

I was speaking for the money lady, kind of a mediator, like they say on the newscasts.

I was just passing behind the second beachhouse, when the door of Mason's place opened. A man stepped out, his eyes wincing against the sudden sunlight. He was thirty years old, dark-haired, five-six and paunchy. His middle rolled gently over his waistband as he moved, which gave him an extra disadvantage against the heat. There was a second man behind him, but he didn't venture outside, preferring to retain the shelter of the doorway. The first man was therefore a visitor, and the shy one Mason.

The fat man said something over his shoulder. Not wishing to get involved with any third parties, I turned immediately into the space dividing the second and third bungalows, for all the world like a passing neighbour. There was a patch of shade there, with a couple of stunted bushes fighting for survival. I sat down behind them, annoyed that I wouldn't be able to see how the two men parted company. However, that was a small price to pay to avoid being spotted, so I waited and watched the road.

Within seconds, the paunchy one went past, not looking in my direction. I waited until he was clear, then sidled back to the opening and peaked around, in time to see him climb into the Toyota, back around and drive off. I was also in time to note the California plate.

Somebody else knew where to find Mr. Mason, and I wondered who he might be, and where he fitted into this little blackmail scheme. Well, I hadn't time to waste on that kind of speculation. Slowly now, I ambled along to Sea Dream, making a great play of reading house plates on the way. If Harry Mason was watching from a window, I didn't want him to do anything precipitate. A man who is expecting unknown executioners is liable to start blasting at any stranger who gets too close. It behoves us strangers to proceed, as they say, with caution.

I spent a long ten seconds studying the wooden name-plate reading 'Sea Dream', then approached the door with slow steps. As I raised my hand to bang on the shutter, a voice growled from the other side.

"What do you want?"

"Looking for Harry Mason," I replied, keeping my voice low.

Pause. Then,

"Who are you?"

"I don't talk to doors," I told him, huffily.

The door swung suddenly inwards, I saw the gun first, the man behind it second. The gun was big, like an old-fashioned frontier Colt, with fresh oil around the cylinder which announced it was ready for work. Harry Mason was a lean, weather-tanned man with tight dark features and eyes like chips of ice. If his continual shifts of expression were anything to judge by, Harry was in a highly nervous state. It was a relief to see that the brown hand cradling the revolver was rock steady.

"Inside," he snapped.

Whatever else he might be, Harry was no professional hoodlum. He didn't even bother to step back, so that he was well clear as I passed. It's funny the way some people imagine that simply holding a gun makes them masters of the earth. As I went by, I kicked him lightly in the shin, knocked up his gun hand, and with a rapid twist, tore it from his grasp. He yelped with pain, and stared at me in frozen fear.

"Relax Harry," I advised, "Nobody wants to hurt you. I just don't like people waving guns at me. Let's all sit down and have a nice chat."

I motioned with the Colt, and he stumbled into the living area, nursing his hand.

"I think you broke a finger," he complained.

"Look at it from my point of view," I urged, as he flopped into a dusty chair, "You were all set to blow holes in my nice manly body, Harry. Don't complain about one finger. Where'd you get this thing anyway? A Wild West museum?"

"Went with the job," he told me, "We used to wear these old gunbelts and holsters, like kind of a uniform. The customers thought they were fakes, but they weren't."

"Ah," I nodded, resting the weapon on a low table beside me, "That would be in the casino you worked in. Palm Springs, did you say?"

"I didn't say," he grunted, "But you seem to know anyway. And you still didn't tell me who you are."

I ignored that, looking around at his temporary headquarters. It was strictly functional, a place to come at the end of a day's vacation, with minimal comforts.

"I hear you're in a lot of trouble, Harry. Like to tell me about it?"

I leaned back, and lit an Old Favourite, all set for a cosy chat. Mason stared at me in frustration.

"Go to hell," he suggested.

"Oh tut tut," I reproved, "No need to be that way with me. No need at all. I might be able to help you. On the other hand, if you really don't want to talk, I could just go away and — "

"Why don't you just do that? Just get the hell out of here, and we'll pretend you never happened."

I sighed.

"You interrupted me, Harry. I wasn't

quite finished. I was going on to say that I'd go to three places I know in Monkton. All I'd do would be to tell the barkeep your name and this address. If there are people looking for you, one of those places will know about it. You wouldn't last the night. Now why don't you stop trying to act like a movie gangster, and tell me what this is all about?"

He looked over at the gun, measuring the distance from where he was sitting. I patted it with my hand, shaking my head at the same time.

"You seem to know a helluva lot already," he grumbled, "How'd you find me? Did she send you? Ellen?"

"It's possible," I admitted, "Now, why should she do that?"

"Don't you know?" he countered, with surprise.

I wagged my head sideways.

"All I have is a sketchy kind of outline of what this is all about. You know how women love to dramatise everything, Harry. I'm a great believer in hearing all sides of the story. How about yours? Oh, and I ought to tell you, I don't have all night to waste on this. If we can't get together, I'd just as soon go and make those visits we were talking about."

"I'll bet," he said sourly, "Well, what is it you want to know?"

I beamed at him with approval.

"All of it. Every tiny bit, right from the beginning. Start with when you first met Ellen."

He hesitated one last time then shrugged.

"Not much to it, happens every day. You know how it is with these rich dames. They got too much money and too much time. They get bored, and they get this itch. So they take a ride out of town, head for the action. Vegas, Miami, the Springs, any place where it's at. And those places, believe it, are waiting for them. I work in a place called the Last Chance Saloon. It's like an old frontier joint, you know, except for the carpets and the air-conditioning — "

" — and the prices," I supplemented.

" — right," he agreed, "We operate a twenty-five dollar minimum stake, even on blackjack, so it's no place for poor people. Anyway, Ellen comes in one night, and I know what she's there for. I've been the route a few times, and I can tell. We kind of get together for a few days, then she takes off. I was sorry when she went, I really liked her."

"When was this?" I queried.

He puckered up his forehead.

"Lemme see, this would have been May. Yup, end of May. Why?"

"Nothing special. I just wondered what took you so long showing up here in Monkton."

Mason glared at me, and when he spoke, his tone was nasty.

"What's that supposed to mean?"

"It means that if you were intending to put the bite on the lady, you took your time getting around to it."

He shook his head, as if to clear it of unwelcome thoughts.

"You think this is my regular style?" he expostulated, "You think I'm one of those creeps who does this all the time. They got a word for guys like that."

"Yes they do," I returned equably, "And from where I sit, I don't see why it shouldn't apply to you."

About to argue some more, he changed his mind, and heaved his shoulders around.

"Think what you like, I never done nothing like this before."

"So why now?" I countered.

"I made a mistake is why. Tried to buck the action in the old Last Chance. At my age you'd think I'd know better, but this guy had a system, and I didn't see how we could fail."

This is an old story around the gambling circuit. No matter what the newspapers try to tell you, about rigged tables and crooked dealers, and all the rest of the fairy tales, the fact is that most gaming houses are strictly on the up and up. The odds are heavily in favour of the house, and they don't have any need for all that elaborate cheating. What would be the point? Nine times out of ten, the gambler is going to lose anyway, without any assistance from electronic devices or slippery fingers. All they have to do is wait, and those profits come rolling over the green baize. In fact, they go to the other extreme, and welcome the occasional big winner. He gives them great publicity, crowing about how he beat the house, and they will provide champagne and a microphone. Let him crow, is their angle. He can have a musical accompaniment, if he wants it, because all he's doing is to bring in more customers, all fresh and dewy-eyed. If he can do it, so can they. The word gets around and, in no time at all, whatever the winner took out of the pot has been replaced three, four times over, by bettors anxious to succeed him.

So, as I say, the management has no need to cheat. What it does have to guard against is people who are out to do a little cheating on their own account, and here the story is very different. They have to be constantly on the alert, for players with their own ideas about what constitutes a fair game. These can include syndicates working against the dealer, sophisticated electrical bugs, and sometimes the straightforward cooperation of a house employee. The last method is the most highly-favoured, because it has the greatest chance of undetected success.

Harry Mason would seem to have employed the cooperation system. And be detected. His employers would be sure to take a grave view of his defection.

"How much did you clip them for, before you were spotted?"

"Almost eighty grand," he replied miserably. "We spread it over almost three weeks."

Three weeks is a long time in that world, and it prompted my next question.

"It must have been a good system if you got away with it for three weeks," I commented, "What went wrong?"

"My jerk partner is what went wrong," he said bitterly, "The guy got too confident, started laying into that old juice one night before he played. We'd been taking it easy up to then. Three, four grand at a time, nothing fancy. The monitors don't pay any attention until you pass five grand, then they really take an interest. This cluck I'm working with, all of a sudden he decided to get greedy, go for the big one. On top of that he gets careless and you can bet they're on to him in no time. Lucky for me, it looks like a solo operation at first. When they take him away to talk it over, I'm away and running. It wouldn't take them long to get the whole story and my life wouldn't be worth a nickel, once that happened."

"When was all this?"

"Day before yesterday. I was running scared, and this was the only place I could think of, where I might get a grip on some stake money."

There was no ashtray within reach, but the scarred wooden floor showed how earlier occupants had dealt with that problem. I ground out the butt under my foot, reviewing what Mason had just told me. So far, everything fitted in with Ellen Ralph's version.

"So you put the squeeze on Mrs. Ralph?" I asked.

He nodded vigorously, looking worried at the same time.

"Yes I did, but don't think I enjoy doing it. This ain't my style at all. I'm desperate. Those guys'll kill me once they catch up."

"Yes they will," I confirmed, matter-of-factly, "Some people might feel they have a right. We got a problem here, Harry. Mrs. Ralph needs a few days to raise the cash. You say you won't wait, but I say you will. You play chess?"

"Chess? There's no dough in chess. Why?"

"In chess, this is what we call a checkmate situation."

He looked cunning then.

"Except I have this extra piece called Mr. Ralph," he reminded, "Once I move him around, I win."

I shook my head sadly.

"Wrong," I contradicted, "Mrs. Ralph has an extra piece, too. Me. If you collect from Mr. Ralph, I take the dough away from you. Not only that, I'll blow the whistle on you. My advice is, forget about the husband. What we have to do here, we have to find you a hole to crawl into, while the lady is putting the money together."

He wasn't really paying attention now. He stopped listening after the part where I'd said I'd take the money from him. For the first time, since he realised I wasn't there to kill him, he showed signs of real hopelessness.

"You'd do that? You'd really do that?"

"Really would," I assured him cheerfully, "Glad to. If it was left to me, I'd just as soon let the Palm Springs crowd have your number, but Mrs. Ralph wouldn't like that. She's the kind of person who'd blame herself if something happened to you. So, I guess it's up to me to keep you alive while she digs up the cash."

He stared unhappily at the floor. Ten minutes earlier, he'd been the dealer. He was the one with the gun and all the cards. Now, suddenly, he had nothing, and he knew it.

"Why can't I just stay here?" he demanded, "It's as good a place as any."

"Wrong. I'm surprised at you, Harry. You won't stay at a hotel, because those are the first places a mob will be looking. But where's the second place? Short-term rental, that's where. Places like this. You might as well be at the Monkton Hilton, and it's a damned sight more comfortable. I know places no-one will look. Get your toothbrush, Harry."

Reluctantly, he drew himself up, and started throwing bits and pieces into an expensive handgrip. It took him less than five minutes, then he snapped it shut and looked at me.

"One other thing, before we go," I said gently, "Who's your friend? I like to know all the players."

"Friend?"

"Tubby guy, dark. He was here in the house, just a few minutes before me. Where does he fit in?"

He'd looked worried again for a few moments, but now his face cleared.

"Him? He's no friend. He owns this place, is all. Paid a little surprise visit to see what kind of a set-up I have. He's been in trouble with the law for not checking, so he says. People sometimes use his places as floating crap games or drug drops or whatever. Nowadays, he's more careful."

"Very sensible," I conceded, "Then he has a name."

"Arthurson. He's Arthur Arthurson,

would you believe?"

I got up, shoving the big revolver inside my shirt, and thankful it wasn't far to walk to the car.

"Let's go."

Harry Mason picked up his case, took a final look around, and led the way out into the evening sunshine.

3

I took Mason to a filling station on the outskirts of town. The owner is an old friend, always glad to let me have the use of the spare room over his storehouse. Then I contacted Sam Thompson, a guy who does occasional work for me, and brought him into the act as nursemaid/bodyguard. He didn't like the idea, and made his usual protest, but then, anything which is remotely akin to work always produces the same reaction in whatever quarter. Thompson has this economy gap, occasioned by a shortfall between his capacity for booze-consumption and his ability to meet the tariffs demanded by the suppliers. From time to time, when the bartenders are beginning to get that certain gleam in their eyes, Sam will undertake small commissions for strictly limited periods, diverting the resultant cash to those areas which will restore the natural rhythm of his existence. When it suits him, he is a very tough and reliable operative, and I knew Harry Mason was in good hands.

The evening was wearing on now, and the sun had finally disappeared on its essential task of making somebody else's life miserable on the other side of the planet. The concrete, steel and plastic city structures scarcely noticed its absence. They'd all had something like fourteen hours in which to stash away plenty of residual heat, which was now brought into play, bouncing its sticky unbreathable way around the city canyons, and promising a difficult night for anyone with any radical ideas about getting any sleep.

Back in the middle of town, I put in my promised call to Ellen Ralph. The phone was picked up on the second ring, and I almost missed the faint clicking sound which occurred just before she spoke. Almost, but not quite.

"Hello," she said guardedly.

"Mrs. Ralph? This is Preston," I announced.

"Who?"

"Preston, Mark Preston," I replied.

"Do I know you, Mr. Preston, or is it my husband you want?"

If I hadn't heard that click her offhand tone would have annoyed me. A bead of sweat ran off the end of my nose, and spilled against the mouthpiece.

"That is Joan Ralph, isn't it? International Cosmetics?"

"No. You have the wrong number," she said coolly, and put down the phone. I waited, listening, and again came that second click.

I sat in a bar, as close to the whirring fan as I could get, and nursed a tall glass of ice-cold beer. So much for Ellen Ralph's assurance that a telephoned report would present no problem. Someone else had been listening, there was no doubt about that. The point was, why? Was her husband for some reason suspicious about what was going on, or did he just automatically monitor all her calls? And if so, why?

No, I reasoned, the latter explanation wouldn't do. If Joe Ralph was in the habit of checking his wife's use of the telephone, then she would certainly know it, and would not have been so quick to agree that I should call her. Therefore, if it wasn't a regular practice, it was a new development in their lives, and that posed the next question. Why?

I stared morosely into the white suds, as though they might suddenly provide an answer. Fine state of affairs. Here was me, making all this progress on the lady's behalf, and not even able to set her mind at rest. Ah, well. If I couldn't do any more in that direction, there were still some dark corners where I wanted to let in some light. I had a few names to play with, names lead to people, and people always have some kind of story. My business is not unlike prospecting for gold. You set out with just a shovel and a mule, and most of the time you wind up with rock. But you have to keep at it, because you know that gold is around there someplace and, every now and then, you strike pay dirt. Most of the places I wanted to look came under the heading of legitimate enterprises, and there isn't a lot a man can do about those at night, but there were a couple of calls I could make before it was time for bed. There was no hurry that I could see, so I didn't mind too much when a couple of Jule Keppler's men gave me the big hello and pulled up chairs. Big Jule occupies an important place in my life. As the town's biggest bookie, he is always very concerned about my continued health and welfare, because I am a substantial contributor to his luxurious lifestyle. Some people regard betting on the horses as sinful, others think it merely foolish. I don't share either of these views. With me, it's more of a legitimate investment. I happen to be one of those fortunate people with access to gold-plated information, and when I hear that a certain horse is not going to be trying very hard, then it isn't too difficult to work out which of the others is going to beat him to the post. Or it may be that a certain jockey is celebrating his twenty years on the saddle, and the others are going to let him walk home. This kind of inside stuff is not available to the ordinary man in the street, so naturally I have to get my money down when it comes my way. It's hardly my fault if some of the information turns out to be unreliable. Why, just the day before, I got this tip about the third at Palmtrees. It seemed the trainer of one nag had this golden-haired little daughter, who suffered from some obscure disease. The only way for her life to be saved was an immediate operation by some leading surgeon in Switzerland. Everyone knew the story, and every other horse in the race was going to run in rubber boots, so that the poor man would be certain to win and save the life of the little 'G.H.D.'.

I don't need a house to fall on me, when I get quality lowdown like that, and I put five centuries on the nose. The end of the tale was that they had to send out people with flares so the horse could find its way home. It seemed the golden haired daughter was actually a peroxide blonde from upstate, and the only operation she needed was a facelift. Anyway, I was in to Big Jule for this yard, and he isn't a man who has a lot of time for hard-luck stories. When his minions parked themselves at my table, it was all very friendly. I've been keeping their boss in style for too many years for him to worry about getting paid. Just the same, I was glad I had that thousand which Ellen Ralph had slipped me.

"Glad I ran into you fellahs," I assured them, "Matter of fact, you could save me a trip."

They looked at each other. "How could we do that?" one asked. I lowered my voice. The place was crowded, and nobody was taking any interest in us, but it was force of habit.

"I have some money for your boss," I explained, "I was going to drop it around to the office tomorrow, but you could take it now."

I palmed five one hundred dollar bills across the table and they disappeared into a massive fist.

"Boss'll appreciate that, Preston. Lucky, us running into you this way. Why don't we all have a beer."

Why not indeed? I told them about the trainer's daughter, and we all had a good laugh at that one. Then they told me about how they kept busy persuading some of Big Jule's errant clients into catching up on their arrears. They found the anecdotes amusing, so had to join in the laughter, but it was what you might call hollow. Then, after a couple more beers, they went on their way, and it was starting to get late.

I had just decided to call it a night when Sam, the owner of the place, turned up at my elbow.

"Man on the phone for you," he explained, "Are you here?"

Sam's very good that way. There are working bars and drinking bars. In working bars I'm always available, but in a drinking bar like Sam's, I prefer to have the choice. Now, I shrugged.

"I guess so," I decided, with reluctance. After all, this might be a red-hot tip about tomorrow's meeting in Palmtrees, and I was in no position to reject vital information.

We elbowed our way through to the counter where the uncradled phone rested. I picked it up.

"Preston," I announced, "Who is this?"

There was a background noise at the other end, as though the caller was also in a bar somewhere.

"You the private eye, Preston?" demanded a man's voice.

"None other," I assured him, "Who're you?"

All I received by way of a reply was the definite sound of someone hanging up. I jiggled the rest up and down, but the line was clear. Sam was back behind his counter by this time, and he cocked an inquiring eye at me.

"Some nut," I told him, crossly.

I'd been about ready to leave anyway, and the mysterious caller had provided the final spur. Taking one last breath of the almost-cool air, I went out into the heat of the night streets. The sky was all black velvet with stars picked out clear and bright, and never a cloud in view. As I unlocked the car door, I took one final look up, and that was when the sky fell in. Something struck me a crushing blow on the back of the head, and the velvet seemed to crumple, while stars jumped crazily around in the creases. There were other images too, the roof of the car, then the door, finally the welcome sight of dry pavement rushing towards my face.

The next thing I knew was a hand shaking at my shoulder.

"Hey, fellah, wake up."

I took no notice. I was fine where I was, thank you very much, stretched out on this comfortable street, and why couldn't people leave a man alone. Fine thing, when —

"Let him rot," said a new voice, "Just another drunk."

"Stand aside there, police," came a barked command.

That was a welcome sound. The police would look after my interests. After all, where a man chooses to rest is his own business, and they would see I wasn't disturbed.

"Hey you," and an even rougher hand grabbed me by the shoulder, pulling me over on my back.

I opened one reluctant eye, to find myself staring into an unfamilliar face, surmounted by a too-familiar cap.

"You sick, or what?" demanded Face.

There was that in his tone which told me he would not go away. I tried to sit up, and there was a jarring pain at the base of my skull, which I grabbed at instinctively.

"Mumble," I said.

"What?"

"Drunk is what he is," pronounced my unknown enemy among the bystanders, "Toss him in the can, officer."

"Not drunk," I managed.

Face sniffed the night air.

"That ain't Chanel No. 5 you've been drinking," he accused.

My head was clearing by the second now. I was half propped against the car, with a uniformed officer kneeling beside me. Behind his head was a blur of faces. I didn't want to tell my story, but at the same time I couldn't risk being thrown into the drunk tank for the night.

"I slipped and banged my head," I explained feebly.

"Oh yeah?"

Knowing fingers probed behind me.

"Like hell you did," accused Face,

"Somebody belted you from behind, is what."

"Here officer, this was beside him."

One of the blurs leaned forward, holding something out. The officer took it, and rummaged at it with his hands.

"Your name Preston?" he demanded.

"Yes," I confirmed.

"Well, this here is your wallet, Mr. Preston. My opinion, you been mugged, Try sitting up, you won't die."

Whether it was the lack of sympathy in his tone, or the fact that my wallet was in his hands, I don't know. Certainly, I contrived to follow his advice. There was some discontented mumbling among the blurs, who now melted away, disappointed. Evidently, they'd been hoping for at least my dying words, and I had no business coming back to consciousness that way.

"That must be it," I was forced to admit, "Somebody must have slugged me."

Face nodded, bored. There were forty muggings per day in that part of town, and he didn't find any reason to get excited about my little predicament.

"Better check the contents," he advised.

The money was gone, naturally. With the five hundred I had left from Ellen Ralph's retainer, plus what I'd been carrying before, I was now some six hundred and forty two dollars out of pocket. A happy thought struck me. What a piece of good fortune that I should have squared myself with Big Jule Keppler before the mugger got to work. Otherwise, I should have been in a very large minus situation.

"What's so funny?" queried Face.

Bored he might be, but that didn't mean he'd fallen asleep.

"They didn't steal the plastic," I explained.

He grunted. I could go along with that, if my monthly summaries were anything to judge by. It was time to leave. Using his strength to lever me, I got to my feet.

"Much obliged, officer, I'll be fine, now."

He hesitated. Strictly speaking, I was a victim, and victims ought to make statements and set up a whole lot of paperwork. The paper would swell an already overstretched system, and find its eventual way into the 'unsolved' category, providing more fuel for the anti-police faction. He didn't want all that hassle, and neither did I. Equally, if he took no action, he was laying himself open to a personal lawsuit from me, on the grounds of dereliction of duty. Luckily, I knew his dilemma.

"Make me a notebook entry," I suggested.

If he noted the incident on his sheet, then the senior duty officer would make a routine contact with me later, and I could confirm officially that I would be pressing no charges. His face brightened.

"Well now, if you're sure. Somebody ought to take a look at that head, though."

"Somebody will," I assured him solemnly.

He made a scribbled entry, gave me a final friendly admonition, and went on his way. I groped my way into the car, and drove very carefully home to Parkside Tower.

The apartment at Parkside is one of the compensations of life. When I started out in this business, I went the usual route of sleeping on the office couch, and it held little appeal. The first time I made a decent score, I spread myself to some high-class living accomodation, and it was the best investment I ever made. In fact, when you came right down to it, it was the only investment I ever made, unless you count my forays into the horse-racing market. The thing was, the customers liked the address. They seemed to think it was more dignified to have their dirty work done by a man with a Parkside Tower address, than by some character from River Street. Same man, same business, but that's the way people are. On a personal level, I appreciated the change of surroundings, and never more so than when I had bruises to nurse, like now.

I spent a few minutes pampering my head, which had now settled down to a steady throb. Luckily, the hair is especially thick at the spot where the mugger applied the pressure, and that probably saved me from a fractured skull. I scowled at the thought of those people. The world was getting to be some kind of a place, when a man wasn't even safe coming out of a respectable joint like Sam's Bar.

After that, I parked myself next to the phone, and put in a call to the Motor Vehicle Bureau. There wasn't anybody on duty at that hour who knew me personally, so I had to go through the routine of quoting my license number, and answering a few questions from some new badge, before he graciously agreed to run the plate on the Toyota I'd seen out at Fisherman's Quay.

The car was registered to one Leonard Shapiro, with an address in Glendale. I thanked the man and hung up. According to Harry Mason, the man I'd seen leaving the beach house had been called Arthur Arthurson, so who was Shapiro? Not that I was going to make too much or it. People borrow each other's cars all the time. If Arthurson was temporarily without transport, there was nothing to prevent him having the loan of a car from his old friend Shapiro. It doesn't always pay to make a great mystery out of every little detail. Most of life's apparent oddities are capable of the most mundane explanations.

Having dealt with the car, I gave my attention to Mr. Joseph Ralph, the big shot financier who listened in to his wife's telephone conversations. There again, I wasn't going to read too much into that situation. A man with a wife who looked like Ellen Ralph might well think it was a good idea to check up on her activities from time to time, especially if it was one of those December and May pairings.

At that time of night, I could think of only one man who might know enough about the mysterious world of tee-vee finance to give me some kind of hint about Ralph. Unfortunately for me, my contact wasn't answering, not unless you counted his cheerful recorded assurance that he'd get back to me in no time at all. Since somebody first came up with the bright idea of the taped message, my life has been littered with these empty guarantees. I sometimes wonder whether the proud owners ever bother to run the tape at all.

Disappointed, I settled back into the chair to review the progress of events since my chat with Mrs. Ralph, who used to be Ellen Brady. Then I got to thinking back to the That Girl Susie show, and trying to recall some to the other members of the cast. It's odd, when you have a bad headache, and your mind is rambling through a kaleidoscope of half-remembered images, the way you can suddenly lose all touch with reality, and —

I woke up with a start. It was two o'clock in the morning, my head pain was now reduced to a dull throbbing, and there was a taste in my mouth like iron filings. I heaved my grumbling way out of the chair, and went to bed.

4

I made it into the office a little before ten. Florence Digby inspected me with her customary frosty care.

"You look awful," she greeted.

"Thanks. Nice seeing you, too," I assured her, "What's on the stove?"

She pretended to consult a notepad on which she scribbles messages. I say 'pretended' because the day hasn't yet dawned when Florence doesn't have total recall of every detail for a thirty-day period. Thirty minutes would not stretch her.

"Mr. Andrew Devlin called, of Devlin Associates. He wanted you to contact him, when you came in."

It was a message and a reproach, all in one. She has a talent for that kind of thing.

"Did he say what he wanted?"

"Not to me, except that he has a matter he would like to discuss with you. A confidential matter. He sounded very correct."

Correct. La Digby always chooses her words with care, and I had come to learn her private system of people categorisation. Mr. Devlin evidently made all the right vowel-sounds, and had known how to speak to a lady on a business matter. At the same time, he was an unknown quantity, and not therefore qualified for a full endorsement. For the moment, she was playing it safe.

"Devlin Associates?" I queried.

She shook her head.

"I haven't been able to learn anything about them, except that the registered address is in the Thorn building."

Right in the heart of the business section, which probably meant respectable. Yes, I could see that on the evidence to date, Mr. Devlin would slot in as correct. I hesitated. Strictly speaking, I was still working for Ellen Ralph, but the situation with Harry Mason should be cleared within the next twenty-four hours, one way or the other. If he agreed to wait for his money, then there was no problem. If, on the other hand, he decided to approach the lady's husband, there was nothing I could do to stop him. Whichever way it landed, my part would be finished.

Which left me.

Thanks to the punks who emptied my wallet the night before, I was facing another cash fluidity crisis. Possibly, the correct Mr. Devlin would be able to help me out. Florence had that polite enquiring expression.

"Can't do any harm to talk to the man," I conceded, and went through into my own office.

I was scarcely in the chair before she had him on the line.

Mr. Devlin, it transpired, had a problem. No, he could not discuss it over the telephone, but he would very much appreciate it if I could call at his office. I hemmed and hawed a couple of times, but finally agreed to drop over around noon. That ought to give me enough time to make whatever progress there was to be made on the Ellen Ralph affair.

It was a reasonable assumption that her husband would be out at his office, since it was already mid-morning, so I put in a call to the house. A man answered,

"Yes?"

Problem. If I were to hang up, and Joseph Ralph was already entertaining suspicions about his wife's activities, I would only make things worse.

"Is Mrs. Ralph there, please?"

"Who is this?" he demanded.

I told him Mrs. Ralph had been selected as one of the lucky ladies to be given our full beauty treatment, at absolutely no personal cost whatsoever. The only requirement was that we reserved the photographic rights at all stages of the course, and —

He'd heard enough by then.

"Mrs. Ralph is away right now, and she won't want your offer when she does come back," he interrupted.

I tried to sound disappointed, and began to try talking him round, but he hung up on me. I stared at the silent telephone for a moment, wondering whether the voice at the other end had belonged to Joseph Ralph, and whether it was true that the lady wasn't at home. The man hadn't been too sharp with me, sounding more bored with the call than anything else. The obvious thing, if Ellen had been there, would have been to let her deal with me direct. Her husband would know that no salesman was going to be put off by a refusal from some third party. On balance, I decided to assume she wasn't there.

I made two more calls, to see what I could learn about Mr. Ralph the financier, but the name produced no immediate reaction. Both my non-informants promised to ask around, and to get back to me if they came up with an answer. All round, I seemed to be making a lot of no progress. My watch announced that it was time to be thinking about Mr. Devlin of Devlin Associates, but first I wanted a quick word with Harry Mason. I'd been intending to call around and have a chat with him, to stall him off for another few hours, but perhaps a telephone call would hold him at least for the next hour or so.

I called the filling station, and got the proprietor.

"Preston," I announced, "That friend of mine, who's staying with you. Think you can get him on the phone?"

There was a slight pause while my question registered.

"You said what?" came the puzzled enquiry, "The guy should be with you by now. It's thirty minutes since he left."

I had one of those nasty moments, when icy fingers seem to be clutching around in the pit of my stomach.

"Just read that to me again," I asked him, "You say he's on his way to me?"

My filling-station friend was finding the conversation as puzzling as I was, as his tone made clear.

"What is it, a rib?" he queried, "You sent for the man, so he come. Listen Preston, I don't have time for games — "

He was beginning to sound peevish, so I hastened to calm him down, and gradually managed to piece together some kind of story. A man had telephoned, asking for Mason, who took the call. He then said that I wanted to see him right away, and took off. He seemed quite excited, as though he'd heard some good news, but he didn't offer any further information.

"Where was Sam Thompson?" I demanded.

"Right here in the diner, having some grub. I told Mason he oughta wait for Sam, but he said no, he wouldn't be away long, and let Sam finish his breakfast. It all sounded kosher, the way he told it to me."

I sat there, fuming. Whether Mason believed the call was genuine or not was a matter for speculation. The bottom line was that I'd lost him. Either he'd gone off to meet someone who was supposed to be me, or else he'd had a wholly different message from some third party, which decided him it was the time to move. I told my mystified contact to tell Thompson to report in to the office fast, and put down the phone.

Outside of myself, the only people who knew where I'd taken Mason were the owner, Thompson, and Mason himself. And yet, somebody had made that call.

The point was, where did they learn the number? Neither of my people had the faintest idea of what this was all about. Even if they wanted to sell me short, which was out of the question, they wouldn't know who to approach. That left Mason himself. He could have tipped somebody off as to where he was, but who? The only person in town who was supposed to know about him was Ellen Ralph, and that lady wasn't taking any calls. In any case, the voice on the telephone had belonged to a man. The only man I knew of was the real estate guy, Leonard Shapiro.

Damn.

Up until a few minutes before, I'd had a fairly straightforward case on my hands. Difficult, yes. Unpleasant, yes. But no worse than plenty I'd handled in the past. Now, with Mason somewhere out there loose, I'd lost control of the game, and I didn't care for that. I didn't care for it at all. If I'd only foreseen earlier that something was about to go wrong. I wouldn't have been so quick to make an appointment with Devlin Associates.

However, there it was. My best move was to go and see the man, get through the chatter as quickly as possible, and set about the new task of locating Harry Mason.

It was difficult to clear my mind, as I negotiated the late-morning traffic. So far, thanks to the punks last night, I was making a profit of dollars nil on the Ellen Ralph thing, and all I had left was trouble. That wasn't any fault of the lady's, but it didn't exactly leave me filled with burning resolve. I almost began to look forward to my talk with Devlin. He probably had a nice little case of employee corruption, stock losses, stuff like that. Besides which, I'd always know I could contact him, which is more that I could say for some clients.

The office was nothing pretentious. Just three rooms on the eighteenth floor, fairly typical of hundreds of small firms up and down the coast. I went in where it said 'please enter', and surveyed the outer fortifications. These took the shape of a bright-faced kid, clearly the proud possessor of a brand-new diploma in business studies, or the like. She looked about twelve years old. I told her who I was, and that Mr. Devlin was expecting me, and she gravely relayed this information into an inter-office communicator, just like the instructor had said. The thing crackled back at her, and she nodded importantly.

"It's the second door," she advised me.

Andrew Devlin was thirty-five years old, and it was time he paid attention to that waistline. He grabbed my hand with enthusiastic pudgy fingers, and seemed genuinely glad to see me.

"Sit down, sit down, Mr. Preston. Yessir, a real pleasure. I never met anyone in your line of business before. Must be quite exciting, I imagine?"

"Sometimes," I conceded, "Mostly it's boring routine."

I'd encountered this kind of reaction before, thanks mostly to the tube. Every night, on every channel, some smooth character could be found, bumping off the opposition like World War Three, with half the dames in town dragging him between the sheets at specified intervals. Nobody ever banged those guys over the head and, even if they did, it was all forgotten by the next sequence.

Mr. Devlin was not to be put off by my disclaimer.

"Yes well," he nodded, "I'm afraid you might find our little problem rather routine. Do you know the company?"

I admitted my ignorance, and he seemed to expect it, launching at once into a potted summary of company activities. They seemed to have fingers in a number of pies on the light industry front, concentrated mostly up-state. During the previous few months they had been bothered by a series of strikes. Mostly, these were of short duration, two or three days at the outside, but they were a nuisance. They cost time and money and, most important, had resulted already on two occasions in a failure to meet delivery deadlines. At first, these stoppages had seemed to be no more than the kind of nuisance which is a normal hazard of business life. They were unpredictable, short term flare-ups, and occurred at random throughout the dozen or so plants with Devlin interest. Although no individual instance had been of special significance, the cumulative effect was that the company was beginning to feel the strain.

"What I'm saying, Mr. Preston, is that this whole thing is being orchestrated, and I want to know who's behind it."

He finished the chatter and waited for my reaction. So did I. It sounded like a complex problem, not the kind of thing a lone hand would be able to crack. On the other hand, I was without visible means of support, and a job is a job.

"I don't know, Mr. Devlin," I confessed, "A thing like this could take weeks, and even then I couldn't guarantee to come up with anything worth having. You say there are a dozen plants, for openers. Whichever one I picked, you can bet the next bit of trouble would be somewhere else."

He nodded brightly.

"Absolutely," he confirmed, "I don't think any useful purpose would be served by hiring you as an operative in any of those locations. You really need access to them all, and here we come to the opportunity. We run a courier service between all our units, kind of a private mail, if you will. The service visits each plant every two days, and the driver spends an hour or so at each stop. It just so happens the man who does that job is leaving us today, and a replacement is needed. I thought you could be that replacement."

He looked at me hopefully, while I scratched my chin.

"That would give me an entry," I mused, as much for my benefit as his, "Even so, I don't hold out much hope. How do you feel about a trial?"

"A trial?" he repeated doubtfully.

"What I mean is, how would it be if I took on this assignment, let's say for one week. That would give me time to look into the set-up, get some idea of whether it's worth your while to keep me on. I don't make a habit of taking on things I can't handle. Give me one week, and I'll make a report. What do you say?"

"That sounds sensible," he conceded, "What would your charges be for such an arrangement?"

I did a rapid calculation, adding in a little something for rent and board.

"I'll do it for twenty five hundred, plus a plane ticket."

Devlin didn't even bat an eye.

"Done," he agreed, "And you'll leave this afternoon?"

I hadn't bargained on anything quite so sudden. From his viewpoint it was a reasonable request. The mail must go through, as they say, and the present driver would be leaving that day. My own position was less clearcut. I had this untidy business with Ellen Ralph and Harry Mason to think about. It was just about over, in any case, because old Harry would be resolving the position, for better or worse, and soon. Still and all, I felt an obligation to my client to be in at the end. In other words, I ought to be around when the balloon went up. Devlin Associates could afford twenty four hours, but Ellen Ralph could not.

"I couldn't leave here today," I told

him, “Best I can manage would be a late flight tomorrow evening. There are other cases I must clear up before I go.”

The plural sounded more imposing. It wasn’t any of his business that I only had one little case, and it wouldn’t do for him to think I was living hand-to-mouth.

He didn’t like it too well, and made a face.

“We’d been hoping for immediate action,” he said, voice rising at the end, to make it a question.

I don’t care for pressure, particularly when there’s no need for it. Devlin Associates had been suffering their problem for many months. I didn’t see that another twenty four hours could make any material difference. At the same time, it was a comfortable assignment, and I could certainly use the money, so I resisted the temptation to snap back at him, and kept my tone concilliatory.

“I appreciate the urgency, Mr. Devlin,” I assured him, “But I have to consider my other clients. How’re they gonna feel if I walk out with the job half-done? Come to that, how would you feel about employing somebody who acted that way?"

He managed a half-grin then.

"I think you've made your point. I'll tell our people in San Francisco that you will report the day after tomorrow. Here is the address."

He handed over a typewritten note, and I stuck it in my pocket. We exchanged a few more words, then I left.

5

The sun was doing its blast-furnace act again, and my hands were slipping on the wheel. There is only one known remedy for this physical disability, which is to remove the hands from the wheel and clamp them around a tall cold glass provided by the proprietor of Sam's. I was standing at the counter, hands in the clamping position, when a familiar voice sounded at my shoulder.

"Been looking for you, Preston. The boss would like a word."

I turned to look at the man they called Stonefoot. He was one of the two collectors working for Big Jule Keppler, and not so many hours before he had relieved me of five hundred of the best. I couldn't imagine what Keppler might want with me, but I didn't like him sending Stonefoot. You have to understand there is nothing wrong with the man's feet. The reason he has this name is because of a lot of unsubstantiated rumours. There was a time back in the seventies when some people decided to move in on Big Jule's operation, and it caused a lot of unrest. Several of these intruders disappeared from view, and the chatter was that they had gone swimming out in the bay, with special handicaps by way of setting their feet in concrete blocks. The man I was now inspecting had reputedly been on hand to supervise the fittings of these hazards, which had been how he came by his name.

Staring now into those flat, expressionless eyes, I suddenly felt the damnedest itching in my feet.

"Keppler wants me? Sure, no problem. Let's just have a beer, and we'll go see him."

Sam set the glass down in front of me, and waited. A hand like a crusher landed on my shoulder.

"No beer. Boss said right away."

I shrugged, and looked at Sam, speaking very clearly.

"Sorry Sam, I don't have time. I'm on my way with my friend here," and I pointed very clearly at Stonefoot, "To see Jule Keppler. If Thompson comes in, tell him I won't be long."

I wasn't really expecting Thompson, but it was all good insurance. If I should take it into my head to do a little unplanned swimming, there were people who would attest to my last known companion.

Beside me, Stonefoot grunted with annoyance, but said nothing as I followed him out to the street. We rode in silence to the greasy spoon which Keppler runs to keep the Internal Revenue happy, then upstairs to the offices where he conducts his real business. There is no betting operation on the premises, because Keppler had been busted a few times in his early years, and learned a lesson. Nowadays, the parlours were scattered around the city, run by Keppler agents, while the man himself remained apart. The place I was in was the nerve-centre, as witness the four telephones on Keppler's desk.

I was less interested in the desk furniture than in the cold reception of the owner.

"Ah," he breathed, by way of greeting.

Stonefoot spoke, for the first time since we left the bar.

"He told people where he was going."

Big Jule raised intimidating eyebrows.

"Now why would you want to do that?" he queried, the voice a grating rasp.

"I'm a bad swimmer," I told him.

There was an impatient snort beside me, but I wasn't bothered about my escort. Keppler was the decision-maker here, the man to watch.

"Wait downstairs," he ordered.

Stonefoot moved silently away, and the door closed. Big Jule leaned back in his chair, surveying me.

"I'm disappointed in you, Preston," he growled, "I had you down for an O.K., then you do this to me."

This? What was this? I hadn't done anything to him at all.

"You lost me," I admitted.

"Yeah? How long we been doing

business, you and me? Ten years? Twelve? I don't figure you."

Whatever it was, I had obviously been tried and found guilty on all counts. This was a side of the man I had never encountered before, and I didn't care for it.

"Suppose you tell me what this is all about?"

He made no reply, but he must have pushed a button under the desk, because at that moment a door on my left opened and a man sidled in. The newcomer had pale sandy hair, with a droopy moustache and eyebrows to match. He had a round white face which looked as if it never saw the sun, and pale watery eyes which were fixed on Keppler.

"This here is Mr. Gumm, my accountant," announced the bookie, "Mr. Gumm likes a quiet life. Most of the time, you wouldn't know he's around, ain't that right, Makepiece?"

Makepiece? I looked at him with new interest. A man with a name like Makepiece Gumm is worth at least one inspection. He didn't return my glance, seeming almost hypnotised by his boss.

"Whatever you say, Mr. Keppler."

Big Jule nodded, evidently accepting the homage as no more than his plain due. The heavily manicured finger he then pointed at me had a thick tracing of black curly hair on the top.

"But don't make no mistakes," he cautioned, "You let Mr. Gumm loose, any place there's reckoning to do, or dough to be counted, and he is just a natural curly wolf. I'm here to tell you, that man can spot a decimal point from two hundred yards."

He beamed at the little man with warm approval, and there was the echo of a frosty smile in the watery eyes of Makepiece Gumm.

"Yessir, a curly wolf." Then, with an abrupt change of tone and direction, "You sent me some paper here last night."

He was talking to me, and he made it sound like an accusation. I wondered fleetingly whether Stonefoot and his companion might have short-changed their boss, but it was unlikely. A collector with sticky fingers is a man with a short life-expectation.

"I sent you five hundred dollars, if that's what you mean," I returned evenly.

Keppler shrugged, ignoring that, and turned to the accountant.

"Tell him the procedure," then, seeing the look of doubt on Gumm's face, "It's O.K. If you don't tell him that, he won't know how we know what we know."

"Very well, Mr. Keppler." The little man cleared his throat. For a moment, I was afraid he might start polishing his spectacles, but instead, he began to recite.

"The numbers are listed, all notes of fifty dollar denomination and upwards. These numbers are then processed through a computer memory bank system, for purposes of possible identification."

"Tell him what that means," interrupted Keppler.

Mr. Gumm was clearly reluctant to give away the secrets of his trade to the passing foot-traffic, but he continued the recitation.

"The serial numbers of notes which are

known to have been stolen are circulated to all major agencies as a matter of routine. In this way — ”

But I'd heard enough. Everybody knows what Gumm was trying to tell me. I understood his hesitance a little better now, because any outfit less qualified to call itself a 'major agency' than Jule Keppler's illegal operation would be hard to find. How he got access to those numbers was a matter of no concern to me. The point was that he had them, and as a result, I was in his office, and things were looking bleak.

"Are you telling me that money I sent you is hot?" I demanded. I wasn't talking to the accountant now, but to Keppler.

He didn't reply to the question directly.

"I don't believe you," he gritted, "How did it go, with you and your pals? What did you say, something like, "Oh don't worry, I know this dumb bookie, I can swing some of the merchandise on him. That the way it was? You never figured I'd spot it, right? What's a few hundred bucks in a busy operation like this? You didn't figure on old Makepiece, right?"

Now that I had the background, I could understand why the man was sore. If Gumm hadn't nailed the numbers, those notes might have been traced back to Keppler, and provided the police department with a bonanza. It would give them an excuse to search all his places, an opportunity they would give their eye-teeth for.

"Listen, I can understand why you're mad," I assured him, "But this is all news to me. I didn't have any idea — "

"The hell you didn't," he cut in, "I'd have bought that, if it had been one note, or even two. You could have picked 'em up legitimate, and passed 'em to me, no harm intended. But it wasn't one, and it wasn't two. It was — er — "

"Six," replied Gumm, "Two fifties and four hundreds."

"Right," grunted his employer, "I don't buy six, Preston. That is no accident."

No, it wasn't, I admitted privately. Ellen Ralph had some explaining of her own to do, but that wasn't my immediate problem. The first task was to get Keppler off my back.

"You say the money is hot. Where did it come from?"

"Bank heist. Two months ago. Cleveland, Ohio."

Clear across the country. No wonder Keppler was upset. We weren't even talking about trouble with just the local police. We were talking about the Federals, the Treasury cops and Lord knows who else besides.

"Give me back the money," I asked, "I'll see it gets replaced within twenty four hours."

"Yes, you will," he stated, "Plus an extra two hundred for pain and suffering. That's just for openers. I want more than that. I want to know where the stuff came from. A man should know who his friends are. And don't give me no arguments, Preston. I'm going to have the whole tale, or you're going to be doing a little of that pain and suffering, and I mean now."

There was no mistaking the menace in his words, and they were more than words. Stonefoot was within call, and probably half a dozen more like him.

I was definitely in a jam, and I didn't like it.

Neither did Makepiece Gumm. He was just the man with access to a memory bank system. This other kind of stuff was outside of his department.

"Er, Mr. Keppler?" he said plaintively.

Keppler didn't even bother to look at him.

"Blow," he dismissed, and the little man scuttled out.

"Well, I'm waiting."

There are times for talking tough, and acting tough. This was not one of those times. I was going to have to talk to Big Jule, and I knew it. At the same time, I wasn't readily going to hand over Ellen Ralph to the tender mercies of his bully boys.

"I had the money from a client," I told him, "A woman. She wouldn't know anything about robbing banks. Let me talk to her, find out where she got the money — "

"Hell with that," he interrupted, "What's her name?"

I tried once more.

"Listen, she has a place out on Boulder Drive, a real money set-up. I'm telling you, she's the kind who'd worry about a parking ticket."

"I'm not talking about parking tickets. I'm talking about five centuries in bad money that you palmed off on me. I'm talking about coppers and courtrooms and real big trouble, and I'm tired of listening to you pussy-footing around. Now, you got a choice. You can either tell me who she is, or you can spend the next twenty minutes bouncing off the cellar walls. I don't get you, Preston. If you're levelling with me, the dame already gypped you out of five hundred bucks. Why should you want a broken leg on top? You're out of time. I got other things to attend to."

He must have pushed one of those hidden buttons again, because the other door opened now, the one behind me. They didn't touch me or even threaten. They simply stood there and waited for the word. At Keppler's say-so, they would take me out and buy me a king-sized steak dinner, or toss me out the nearest window. To them, it was all straightforward routine. Well, I'd tried, and this was no time to be a hero. I wasn't going to be of any use to Ellen Ralph or anybody else, if I was all strapped up in a hospital for the next month.

"Get them out and I'll tell you," I capitulated.

Jule Keppler shrugged and waved a hand. The praetorian guard melted away, and the door closed softly.

"The name is Ralph, Ellen Ralph," I told him, "She used to be Ellen Brady, the tee-vee star. Believe me, that lady . . . "

But he motioned me to be quiet.

"This Ellen Ralph, is she married?"

"Yes," I confirmed, "But her old man doesn't rob banks, either. His name is Joseph Ralph, and he's what they call an angel. One of those people who puts up the finance for new television shows. I don't know how she — "

"Joe Ralph," he muttered.

For the first time since I entered the room, the threat was gone from his brow.

Instead, he was deeply thoughtful, and he stared at the top of his desk, ignoring me.

For my part, I was wondering how it came about that the bookmaker should ever have heard Ralph's name before. Their worlds scarcely coincided. Finally he spoke, and his words were barely audible.

"Preston, you were in trouble when you came in here, but that was nothing to what you're in now. You're messing with Joe Ralph, and I don't want any part of it. Here."

He took some bills out of a drawer, and flung them towards me. I managed to catch one, and let the others flutter slowly to the floor, while I watched his face. He was still angry, but there was a new expression in his eyes, an expression I'd seen too often not to recognise it. They call it fear.

Joseph Ralph was no longer Joseph Ralph. Suddenly, he was Joe Ralph, and the name made Big Jule Keppler afraid.

"What's so important about Ralph?" I ventured.

Keppler shook his head, as though that simple action might clear it of unwelcome thoughts.

"I don't mess with those people," he replied mysteriously, "Pick up that money, and get out of my office. You owe me seven bills, as of now. I'll take it in cash, and I'll take it quick. It's my guess you're already dead, so you ought to get settled up."

The menace was gone from his tone, and that unsettled me just as much as the words. Bending quickly down, I scooped up the tainted money, and shoved it into a pocket. Then I turned on my heels, and went out. Stonefoot watched impassively as I passed him at the head of the stairs, and I was deep in thought as I emerged into the blistering heat of the day.

6

The first thing I had to do was to get rid of the stolen bills. Stopping off at the bank, I locked them away in my deposit box, and watched thankfully as the steel grille closed behind me. In the few minutes since I'd left Keppler's place, I had been doing some rapid thinking.

Ellen Ralph had given me that money in good faith, I decided. For all she knew, I could have gone straight from her house and deposited the money. If I'd done that, the numbers would have been spotted at once, and I'd have been picked up by the law, who would know very quickly how the cash got into my possession. That would take them straight to Ellen, and then to her husband. She had nothing against me, a total stranger, and if she was out to cause trouble for Joseph, now Joe, there were a dozen ways she could have done it, without involving me.

As it turned out, I'd been lucky. Half the money had gone straight to Keppler, and the mugging fraternity had taken charge of the rest. It gave me a feeling of perverse satisfaction to think of those people. As soon as they started passing the cash, somebody somewhere was going to spot it. They might have got away with mugging me, but they wouldn't be so lucky with a charge of unexplained possession of stolen treasury bills. They wouldn't even be able to say who they robbed, because a mugging is no occasion for swapping visiting cards. I was just a face who came out of a bar one night, and they probably wouldn't know me again, even if we met face to face. In an odd way, the streets had done me a favour, because I'd have been trying to pass that money myself within hours, with the results I didn't care to dwell on.

It was in the elevator, on the way up to the office, that a different explanation came to me.

"Are you getting out, or not?"

A peevish voice beside me, brought me back to the present. A tubby red-faced man was bristling at me, and pointing at the open doors.

"Three," he announced, "You pushed three. Right?"

"Oh. Right."

I stepped out, and the doors closed behind me on an irritable monologue about people who couldn't make decisions. It was no time to be arguing with strangers on elevators. There were more important things to think about. Such as my new theory about how I collected the lump now nicely settled at the back of my head.

Street mugging had become such an everyday part of life that everyone takes it for granted. No explanations are sought or even contemplated. It's nothing personal, anymore than a thunderbolt crashing through the roof. The victims are not people, not individuals, they are merely faces who happen to have something of value on their persons. That is the basic relationship between the muggers and the victims, and there is nothing deeper involved. The guys who slugged me had never heard of Preston M and wouldn't have been interested if they had.

But supposing they had?

Suppose the attack was not the unplanned, mindless, casual affair I had assumed? In the light of my recent talk with Keppler, there was a new dimension to be considered, and the more I thought about it, the more I liked it. The assault could have been for the simple purpose of recovering that stolen money, to prevent it from coming to light. If that was the case, then the man behind it was probably Joe Ralph, and the only way he could know about me would be from his wife.

I was warming to the idea now, and I didn't like the way my thoughts were leading me. There was no way Ellen Ralph was going to announce our little exchange to her husband. "Oh, by the way, I gave a thousand dollars to a private investigator, so that you wouldn't find out that I've been sleeping around." That is not the kind of informal chit-chat which gets handed out to husbands.

No. Joe Ralph had missed the money, and put the squeeze on Ellen. She must have told him she'd given it to me, probably making up some tale about the reason. That could explain why I hadn't been able to talk to her, when I called in to report. If her old man was all excited about the missing money, he'd naturally want to know who she was talking to. But his prime concern was to get his property back, and that involved taking it from me.

Then I recalled the man who had called me at Sam's the previous night, and hung up when I answered. At the time, I'd written him off as some kind of nut, but now I had a new thought. It doesn't take a genius to find out that Sam's is my favourite waterhole, anybody in town will tell you. But it's a busy place, and you can't just go around bopping everybody on the head until you find one by the name of Preston. At the same time, if you're setting out to rob a man, you don't go into a public place, asking for him by name. What to do?

You make a phone call to the public place.

It's no more complicated than that.

You make a call, and ask for the party by name. The party answers the phone, and you have people in the place, watching. Then, once the man has identified himself, your people follow him outside and belt him over the head.

As all these flights of fancy flashed through my mind, I was opening the door of the outer office. Florence Digby's face was as imperturbable as ever.

"Ah, Mr. Preston. Right on time."

"For what?" I grouched.

"Why, for Mr. Thompson," she trilled, "He only got here about five minutes ago, and I told him he should wait."

Good. That would put an end to all my fanciful theorising for the next few minutes. Sam had a few questions to answer.

"He's in there?"

I jerked a thumb towards my office. Florence nodded.

"I couldn't have him in here, wasting my time. Besides, he tends to poke into everything, and this is supposed to be a confidential undertaking. He can't do any harm in there."

Which may sound innocuous enough to the untrained ear, but my ears have been trained for years in listening out for La Digby's little ice-picks. What she was saying was that she did all the work, and the only equipment on view in my own room was the telephone.

I gave her one of my very thin grins to acknowledge the sally, and went through. Then I changed my mind, turning in the doorway.

"The new client is Andrew Devlin, of Devlin Associates," I told her, "I'll probably get started on it late tomorrow, so maybe you should open a file. They operate mostly up-state, so I'll be leaving the place in your care for a few days, at least. First, I have to wrap up this thing with Thompson."

She nodded, made a note, and got back to her work. I closed the door behind me, and stared unlovingly at the gnarled features of Sam Thompson, who was sprawled out in my chair.

"Shift the butt, and start talking," I instructed.

He gathered up various limbs and

hauled himself out of the chair. In two strides, he made it to the visitor's seat, which disappeared under his mass.

"You know as much as I do," he grumbled, "All I know is, I'm sitting in the diner, then they tell me you sent for Mason, and he took off."

"You didn't go after him," I accused.

"Why would I?" He looked mildly surprised, "You're the man paying the tab. You sent for the guy, and he went. If you'd wanted me, you'd say so. Right?"

I dumped myself down in the chair, frowning.

"And it didn't even cross your mind the call might be a phoney?"

Heavy-lidded eyes stared at me uncomprehendingly.

"Now how could that be?" he demanded, "We were hiding the man, for his own protection. Nobody in town knew where he was, except you and me. If he said it was you on the phone, why wouldn't it be? Anyways, the first thing I knew, the man was gone. Then you called, and I came straight back to town. Course, I figured it out, since."

I listened patiently. There is nothing wrong with Thompson in the brain department, so long as it isn't fuddled with the good brew.

"Tell me."

He nodded, and put up one of his massive hands, to tick off points with the sausage fingers.

"We can forget the people at the filling station. They don't know Mason, and they don't know nothing about Mason. To them, he's just a face. Yes?"

"Get on with it."

"That leaves you and me. You say it wasn't you, and you should know. That brings it down to me, and Preston," he wagged an enormous digit at my nose, "Even if I wanted to sell the guy out, and you with him, I wouldn't know who was buying."

None of this was getting us anywhere. Mad as I was with the situation, and that involved Thompson, it never for a moment entered my head that he would betray me.

"Come on Sam, we're neither of us getting any younger."

"O.K." He settled back, clearly satisfied at this confirmation that I entertained no suspicion of him. "Mason tipped off somebody himself."

"The call came from outside," I reminded him.

"This morning," he confirmed, "Yes, that's right. What I'm saying is, he must have told this third party where to call him."

I'd managed to work that one out for myself, though I couldn't for the life of me imagine why Mason would do anything so foolish.

"How could he do that?" I challenged, "You were with him every minute of the time. Or, you were supposed to be."

"Right," he confirmed, "Stick with him, you said, and I stuck with him. Except when he took a bath."

"There's a telephone in the bathroom?"

I couldn't keep the disbelief out of my tone. At the place I'd left these two, the bathroom itself was something of a luxury. It was inconceivable there'd be a phone.

"No. Not in the bathroom," he agreed heavily, "The Ameche is stuck on the wall in the passage. He could have made the call from there. In fact, that's the only chance he had."

"You weren't watching him," I accused, childishly.

The contour map which was his face creased into several more gorges.

"No, I didn't watch him," he growled, "The guy was buck naked when he went out of the room. Course, if I'd been a real smart detective, like some people, I'd have figured it out. I'd have said to myself, 'I'll just bet he's going out there to tip off somebody where they can find him. Or, maybe he's going to make a run for it. There's a lot of people strolling around the highway in the middle of the night with nothing on.' But I'm just not that smart. If a man takes off all his clothes and tells me he's going to take a bath, I'm just dumb enough to believe him."

Despite my annoyance, I couldn't resist chuckling at the woebegone expression on his lugubrious features. Thompson was quite right, and I was merely being petulant.

"You're right," I capitulated, "Anybody can be smart after the event. I'm not blaming you, Sam, not really. I'm just mad at Mason, and I'm making noises."

"Then I get paid, right?"

"You do."

I pushed some bills across to him, doing some quick calculations at the same time. So far, this simple little job had cost me well over two hundred smackers out of my own pocket, not to mention the loss or the useless money Ellen Ralph had given me. Add to that the extra two hundred Big Jule Keppler had charged me for his pain and suffering, and I was out fourteen hundred bucks plus. I'd achieved this magnificent loss in less than twenty four hours, and the realisation did nothing for my ego. If anyone in Washington was to find out, I could find myself drafted on to the space missile programme. They can use people with that kind of talent up there, but where I lived it was a no-go philosophy.

Somebody was going to have to make

up the shortfall, and the only somebody with that kind of money was my client, the inaccessible Ellen Ralph. Which reminded me again about her husband.

"Ever heard of a man named Ralph, Joe Ralph?"

Thompson finished stuffing the money into a pocket, and gave his attention to this new problem.

"Ralph?" He closed his eyes, and looked for all the world as if he'd fallen asleep. I waited while he ran the name through his private system. Finally, he shook his head, "No Ralph. Why would I know him?"

"Just tossing pebbles," I admitted, "I was with Keppler an hour ago, and the name seemed to worry him."

There was animation on his face when he heard that.

"I'll tell you this, Preston, I never heard of the guy, but if he worries Jule Keppler, he scares the hell out of me."

His reaction was natural, and pretty much in agreement with my own. Big Jule was a powerful man in the city, and he hadn't gotten that way by yelling for his ma when the going was rough. Thompson was on his feet now, and clearly getting ready to leave.

"Any point in me nosing around for old Harry?" he queried.

I shook my head.

"I wouldn't even know which direction to point you." I admitted, "I don't have the smallest idea what's going on. The man Ralph is a puzzle, but I don't think it would be very smart for you to go digging around in his area."

"That one," he assured me pointedly, "I already figured out for myself. I don't mess with people who make Keppler nervous, not for the kind of money you pay me. In fact,"he added thoughtfully, "Not for any kind of money at all."

He was absolutely right, and I didn't blame him one bit.

"This thing begins to sound like a dead letter. I can't raise my client, and Mason has gone to ground. There's nothing more you can do right now, Sam." Then I remembered my new assignment, "Oh, by the way, I'll probably be going out of town for a few days, starting tomorrow. Call me in the morning, and I'll let you know if there's anything you can be doing while I'm away."

"Kay," he confirmed, and shambled out.

They say a drowning man will clutch at a straw. The only straw I had now was a name, Leonard Shapiro, so I clutched at it. I asked Florence Digby to put through a call to the real estate firm run by Arthur Arthurson. When she made the connection, I picked up the phone.

"Mr. Arthurson, please."

There was a pause. Then a woman's voice.

"Mr. Who?"

"Arthurson," I repeated, "Arthur Arthurson. I do have the right number, don't I?"

"That is the name of the company," she confirmed, "But Mr. Arthurson has been dead for thirty years. If you'll tell me the nature of your enquiry, I'll put you through to someone who can help."

About to ask for Shapiro, I thought better of it.

"No, my mistake. Goodbye."

I put the phone down on what must have been a very puzzled woman, and stared at the ceiling. Two minutes earlier, Arthurson had been a man who happened to borrow a car from somebody called Leonard Shapiro, which was no big deal. Suddenly, he was long-dead Arthurson, which meant that Harry Mason had deliberately misled me about his visitor of the day before. No, I corrected, that wasn't necessarily true. Mason had told me the man's name was Arthurson, that much was right, but maybe somebody had told Mason the same thing. Maybe he really believed the man was Arthurson. After all, he was a stranger in a strange city. If he rented the place at Fisherman's Quay from the firm of Arthur Arthurson, he wouldn't have any reason to doubt that he would be dealing with the boss man. And if that was the case, it meant that somebody had fed old Harry a tale from the outset. Somebody by the name of Leonard Shapiro.

Up until then, Shapiro had simply been a man who happened to own a blue Toyota, which is not yet a federal offence. Now, he was a man in his own right, with something interesting to tell me about Harry Mason. I was glad of the sixth sense which had prompted me to put down the telephone. It wouldn't have done at all for me to have announced myself that way, which would only have tipped off Shapiro that I was interested in him.

Which I suddenly was.

Going through to the outer office, I began to rummage in the telephone directory to see if the name was listed. There were two Shapiros, Leonard; one Shapiro L., and an L.T. Shapiro Ltd. I quickly scribbled down the details on all four, and was on my way back to my own room when the phone blatted. Pausing in the doorway, I looked across at La Digby when she answered. Cupping her hand firmly over the mouthpiece she said:

"It's a woman, asking for you. She won't tell me her name. Sounds worried."

"O.K. Put her on."

I made it to the desk in three strides, and picked up plastic.

"Preston."

"Oh Mr. Preston, everything's gone terribly wrong," sobbed the voice at the other end, "Can you come and see me right away?"

Sobs and all, there was no mistaking the tones of Ellen Ralph. Maybe now I'd get some answers.

"Can't we talk on the phone?" I countered.

"No," she refuted, "Please do come. I'm at the Falcon Hotel. Please."

She was clearly very distressed, and I didn't argue any longer.

"On my way," I assured her, "What's your room number?"

"Er, just a minute, Six-O-Five. I'm registered under Brady."

"Ten minutes."

I cut off, thinking. Until she made that call, Ellen Ralph had been incommunicado, which was probably her husband's doing. Somehow the situation had changed, and she was now running scared, and booked into a hotel under another name.

If she was trying to hide from her husband, it had been a pretty dumb move to revert to her old name. He would have to be nine-tenths of an idiot, not to think of that one. And anybody who puts fear into a man like Jule Keppler is no kind of an idiot at all.

I was halfway to the door when I had second thoughts, and went back to the desk, sliding open the drawer where I keep the spare thirty-eight. I checked the clip, and stuck the cold metal inside my waistband. It wouldn't remain cold for long, not in this weather. And neither would I, I thought miserably. Outside, it would be about four hundred in the shade, and I'd be the only man in town wearing a buttoned jacket. It was either that, or run the risk of being arrested on sight by any passing uniform. The police have this allergy to people who walk around with the hardware sticking out of their pants.

Florence eyed me quizzically.

"Won't you be too hot, all buttoned up like that?"

"Calling on a client," I told her loftily, "I like to make a dignified presentation."

That woman can concentrate more derision into one sniff than anyone else I know.

7

The Falcon Hotel is one of those plastic, chrome and glass structures which seem to infest every major city these days. You could pick up the whole thing and dump it down in Phoenix, Arizona or Paris, France or maybe Timbuctoo for all I know, and no-one would notice the difference. A vast and soulless place, with acres of shiny flooring on which your shoes will not skid, merging into huge public areas with more acres, this time of carpeting, which will quickly absorb the sound of a falling hundred-dollar bill. No-one knows anyone else, and the whole scene is like a gigantic waiting-room at the dentist's, just another shared pain in the great universal joke which is defined as humanity. Sometimes I think those places are run for the benefit of the staff, and certainly a lot of the staff would subscribe to that view.

But, for somebody in my line of work,

the Falcon Hotels of this world have their good points. They are totally and whole-heartedly committed to anonymity. Nobody knows who you are, and nobody cares. With a transient population of two thousand plus people, a face is just a face, and let's leave it at that. Ask any sneak-thief, dip-artist, or any of the other forms of hustler, who are guaranteed a quiet, trouble-free living, as long as they maintain a low profile.

I made my anonymous way to the elevators, and was soon at the sixth floor, studying the directional arrows for my number. In no time, I was rapping at the door of 605.

Almost at once, a woman's voice replied.

"Yes?"

"Preston," I announced, keeping my face close to the wood, "Calling on Miss Brady."

It took her several seconds to undo all the bolts and sliding chains — for the greater comfort and convenience of our patrons — and then the door opened half an inch. A quick inspection, and it was flung wide.

"Oh Mr. Preston. Thank God you're here."

I smiled encouragingly, and went inside. Ellen Ralph closed the door quickly, and stood in front of me, doing her best to return the smile. It must have been painful for her, when you take account of the great blue bruise, now beginning to yellow, on the right side of her face. To avoid staring at it, I dropped my gaze.

"Come in, come in." she urged, "Can I get you anything, a drink, some coffee?"

Her hands kept jerking around, while she tried to make like a hostess, and she was plainly one troubled lady.

"No thanks," I said, keeping my voice soft, "Why don't we both sit down, Mrs. Ralph, so we can talk."

As though glad that an important decision had been made, she bobbed her head up and down, and collapsed into a chair by the window. Next to the chair was a table, and on the table was a bottle. Without seeing the label, I couldn't be certain whether it was gin or vodka, but since it was now only half-full, I doubted whether my hostess could tell either. With my client's nervous state, it was important that I should convey a sense of calm and order. I sat down unhurriedly, pulling out my Old Favourites, and setting fire to one, before I broke the silence.

"Well now, Mrs. Ralph, perhaps you'd better start telling me what this is all about."

She nodded vigorously, as though in complete agreement, but still said nothing. I put on my look of polite enquiry, and waited.

"It's so hard to know where to begin. So much has happened. I — I — "

The voice trailed away, and she stared down at clasped hands, where I could see the fingernails beginning to bite into flesh.

"Start at the beginning." I encouraged, "Take it from where I left your house yesterday evening. Your husband was about due home. What happened when he came in?"

She made a great effort to compose herself, and launched into the recital.

"At first, nothing," she reported, "Joe came in, had his vodka martini with me — it's a routine, you see — then he said he had some work to do in his study before dinner. He often did that, so I went into the kitchen and got on with the preparing, and then he came storming in there. I'd never seen him that way before, so upset, almost out of control. He'd found out the money was missing, the thousand dollars I gave you, and he was beside himself. He took me completely by surprise, shouting questions and accusing me. I'm afraid that I must have looked guilty from the start."

She paused for a moment, still with a look of surprise, even at the recollection. I didn't get it. It seemed to me that she ought to have expected the man to notice, when a large sum like that went missing.

"But you'd had some time to think about it," I reminded her gently, "Surely you must have realised, when you took the cash, that your husband would be bound to spot it? Didn't you have some kind of cover story ready?"

She shook her head, and a piece of hair dislodged itself from above one ear, trailing across her eyes. She pushed it away impatiently as she replied.

"No, not really," she denied, "He always had a lot of money in the study, tens of thousands at a time, and it never even occurred to me that he might count it. I thought I could withdraw a thousand from the bank next day, and replace it. Joe would never know anything about it. That was what I thought, but I was wrong. Horribly wrong."

The words caught in her throat, and one hand flew to her mouth as she drew in a deep breath, fighting back another outbreak of the tears which had already left streak-marks on her cheeks.

I sat quietly until the crisis was past. It would obviously take very little to push Ellen Ralph over into hysterics, and I hadn't gone there to be a nursemaid. Two or three deep breaths later, I tried again.

"About the money," I prompted, "Didn't that ever strike you as odd? I mean, not many people keep large sums like that around the house. Why did he do it?"

She hesitated before answering, reluctant even at that stage to betray the trust of the man she was married to.

"I don't know whether I ought to tell you," she stammered, "It might get Joe into trouble, you see."

"Not from me," I denied, "I'm not with the police, don't forget. Whatever you tell me is confidential."

It seemed to reassure her sufficiently for her to continue with the story.

"Yes, well, I certainly hope so. You see, the money was really for tax evasion. It's not what you'd call being criminal, not exactly. I mean, after all, everybody cheats the Internal Revenue, don't they? And, in any case, it wasn't Joe who was doing it, not directly. He was simply helping out friends of his. I couldn't see there was any real harm, not the way he explained it to me."

I almost wished good old Joe had been there, to explain it to me, but I would have to make do with the explanation at second hand.

"You're going a little too fast for me, Mrs. Ralph," I admitted, "These friends of Joe's, where did they get the money in the first place?"

"Why, from business," she replied, as though that covered the whole enquiry, "You see, what happens is, a company makes a certain cash profit, and they only declare part of it to the Revenue Service. That way, they avoid paying tax on the rest. Then they give it to Joe, and he invests it for them. As he told me, he doesn't have any way of knowing where the money comes from, not in any legal sense, so what he's doing isn't really wrong. It's just very confidential."

She was clearly anxious that I should understand that, and I was a little anxious about it myself, but for very different reasons. The cleverness of Joe Ralph's story was that it had the ring of authenticity. There are plenty of people who are doing exactly what he described to Ellen, and the I.R. Bureau employ an army of agents whose purpose in life is to try tracking them down. They even have a word for it. Skimming, is what it's called, and it costs the country hundreds of millions of dollars per annum in lost revenue. I had to hand it to Ralph. Nobody regards cheating on the income tax as a real crime. By using this partly-acceptable device for covering the shifting of hot money, he was showing a neat appreciation of a shadowy area in the national conscience. Crime is out, but cheating the government is a different conception entirely.

As for Ellen Ralph, this was no time for me to be disabusing her of her spouse's small deception.

"O.K. well, that explains where the money comes from," I continued, "Suppose you tell me what happened then? I mean, after your husband accused you?"

"Well," and she was more composed now, "It was just awful. I mean, he took me completely by surprise, you see. It wasn't only that he realised that the money was gone, but it was this dreadful anger. He was like somebody I'd never met before, a complete stranger. I tried to tell him that I'd borrowed it to spend on clothes, just as a short-term loan, but he wanted to know the name of every store I'd visited, wanted to see the stuff I'd bought. I couldn't keep it up. In the end, I had to tell him the truth. He — " and her hand probed tenderly at her damaged face, " — He hit me. I think it was the shock more than the pain, that broke me down. All the time I've known him, he's never lifted a finger against me. Then, suddenly . . . this."

Knowing what I now knew about the missing bills, I could almost sympathise with Joe Ralph. There he was, carefully nursing all that hot money, with every law enforcement agency trying to track it down, and his wife was out on the town scattering the stuff like confetti. He would want to know, and fast, exactly where every bill had landed. It must have come as almost a relief to know that it all went to one man. Me. Within hours, he had located me, had me banged over the head, and recovered his property. It must have been quite a shock, when he found I'd already disposed of five hundred. Which, in it's turn, posed another unwelcome question in my mind. Once he discovered the deficiency, why hadn't he sent his goons back to ask me about the rest?

But that would have to wait, for the moment. The immediate concern was to get the rest of the story from Ellen Ralph.

"You said you told him the truth," I prodded, "You mean you told him about Mason?"

She nodded miserably.

"I was so shocked, almost hysterical, I'm afraid. It all just poured out, almost before I knew what I was doing."

"Hmm."

Not so good. Not so good for her, for openers, and probably even less good for Harry Mason. The missing Harry Mason.

"Then what happened?"

"Joe wanted to know where he could find Harry, and of course I couldn't tell him. He said there were ways of finding people, and he was going to call in some private detectives of his own. He made a phone call, and two men came to the house very quickly."

"Did you catch the name of the firm?" I queried.

"No. Joe said they were there to guard me, in case you or Harry tried to contact me. He wasn't going to have me letting anybody else know that he was aware of what was going on. I was to stay in the house until he said otherwise. It was then that Harry called."

"Ah."

That would have been when Sam Thompson thought the man was taking a bath. Things were beginning to fit together.

"Well, go on," I urged.

"One of the detectives answered the phone. When he told Joe it was a man named Harry asking for me, Joe told me to answer it, and to find out where he was. I — I did as he said, but Harry couldn't tell me. Or wouldn't, I wasn't certain. He said all he knew was that the place was a filling station. With him being a stranger in town, he couldn't say exactly where it was. All he could tell me was the telephone number."

That made sense. There was no way Mason could have identified the locality, and it would have made me suspicious if

Ellen Ralph had said anything different.

"Your husband took the number, naturally?"

"Snatched it out of my hand," she confirmed.

"Why did Mason call? What did he want?"

"He said he didn't trust you, and I needn't think I was going to get away with anything by having him practically kidnapped. I had only twenty-four hours to come up with the money, and nothing had changed. That was all he said."

I wondered whether Mason would have been quite so cocky, if he'd realised the injured husband was a party to the call. As it was, he'd betrayed himself by giving out that phone number.

"Did you ever call him back?" I asked casually.

"No. They wouldn't let me use the phone," she denied, "And besides, I wouldn't have had any reason. The fact that Joe now knew all about it didn't really change anything. Harry was threatening to tell him the next day, today that is, so it only meant that he knew a few hours earlier."

From her point of view that was true, and I could see that. Whether the newly-explosive Joe Ralph would have taken such a dispassionate view was open to doubt. But, she'd somehow escaped the restraint of the bully boys, and could have warned Mason since. After all, she'd had no problem about telephoning me.

"Why did they let you go?" I asked sharply.

She looked surprised.

"They didn't," she refuted, "Joe left the house late last night, and I haven't seen him since. Those two detectives, if that's what they were, stayed all night. I went to my room and waited, then I climbed out of my window at six o'clock this morning, and ran away. That's how I got to this place. I went straight to bed, and then, when I woke up I called you."

She left out the part about sinking all that booze, but I let it pass.

"I see. But you didn't call Mason this morning."

Again, there was that puzzled expression.

"No. Why do you keep asking me that?"

"Because somebody did," I explained, "Somebody called him, at that number he gave you. He claimed the call was from me, and took off. My man lost him, and, as of now, I don't have the slightest idea where he is. Tell me, what made you say, just now, that those men might not be detectives. What reason did you have for doubting it?"

She shrugged, and that stray piece of hair did its falling act again.

"They didn't act like employees. It was more as if they knew him, somehow. And I heard one of them call my husband Joe. That's not exactly normal between strangers, is it, not when one is supposed to be employing the other?"

"No," I agreed, "Well, where do we go from here, Mrs. Ralph? What do you want me to do?"

Her shoulders slumped forward, and I thought for one anxious moment she was going to wilt on me.

"I was hoping you'd be able to do something, anything, but it's all hopeless now, isn't it? If Harry Mason's got away from you, I don't see what there is to be done. My husband knows the whole story, and I guess that's the end of just about everything."

It wasn't logical that I should feel sorry for her. After all, if she hadn't deliberately gone out playing footsie with Mason in the first place, the whole blackmail dodge would never have arisen. She'd been unlucky in borrowing that money from her husband's private stock-pile, but from where I was sitting, the main loser was me. I had wound up with a fee of dollars nil, plus a bump on the head, with more unpleasantness on the calendar when Joe Ralph wanted to know what I'd done with the missing five hundred.

All the same, there was something in her hopeless posture which called up whatever remains of my protective male instinct.

"Does anyone else know you're here?" I asked.

She looked up at me.

"Why, no. What makes you ask?"

"Just thinking. If your husband starts

looking for you, it shouldn't take him long to find you. Using your single name wasn't very smart, you know. I think it might be as well if I have a friend of mine come and sit with you. You'll be safe with him."

"What will you be doing?" she wanted to know.

That was a question which was also bothering me, but this was no time to sound indecisive.

"I'll be out and around," I announced authoritatively, "Don't forget, I now know about what kind of money your husband keeps in his study. That ought to give me something of an edge. He's mad at you, and he has every right to be, but it doesn't have to be the end of the world. Let me see what I can do."

I got up to leave, and after a brief hesitation, she rose to her feet, pushing hair away from her eyes.

"I guess I don't come out of this too well," she muttered.

"Lady, one of the first things you learn in this business is not to make judgements about people. People are just people, and that's all they are. If everybody behaved like Goody Two Shoes, the world would probably cease to revolve. Besides which," and I produced one of my reassuring manly grins, "How would anybody like me make a living?"

At the door, I said:

"My man's name is Thompson, Sam Thompson, and I'll have him here as quickly as possible. Oh," and there was one question I'd almost forgotten, "By the way, how did Mason come to rent that place down at the Fisherman's Quay? Did he arrange it by himself, or were you involved at all?"

The unexpected nature of the question brought her temporarily out of her misery.

"Why, I suggested someone to him. He didn't want a hotel, you see, and he had to have somewhere immediately, so I gave him the name of somebody I knew. What makes you ask?"

"Just a detail. What name did you give him?"

"A man named Shapiro, Leonard Shapiro."

"Close friend of yours? Or your husband's?"

She shook her head.

"Not close, certainly. Just a man I happened to meet through Joe one time. I still don't see why you're asking. What does it matter? Oh, I see what you mean. Harry will have left without paying his rent, and Len will hold me responsible."

Such a thought had never entered my head, but it certainly gave me an out.

"It's an easy way to lose a friend. You might like to bear it in mind."

"You're very thorough aren't you? Thank you."

"All part of the service."

I left her there, and went out feeling very thorough.

Or thoroughly something.

8

I called the office from the pay-phone in the lobby, and told Florence Digby to get Thompson over to the Falcon Hotel, plus artillery. She made a careful note of the room number, then said:

"Is that it?"

"That's it," I confirmed.

"I shall see to it at once. There is a message for you, from the police department. Sergeant Randall is anxious to get in touch. Will you call him?"

Randall? I didn't like the sound of that, at all. Detective Gil Randall, to give him his full nomenclature, is one of the formidable combination of Rourke and Randall, the much-feared spearhead of the Homicide Squad.

"What does he want?"

"I really can't imagine," she assured me frostily, "Mr. Randall is very frugal with his confidences. In that respect, he often reminds me of someone else

I could mention."

I made a face in the cracked glass on the wall.

"All for your own good," I retorted, "What you don't know can't get you in trouble. Did he say it was urgent?"

"He never says anything else."

"O.K. well, I'll call him first chance I get. Is that it?"

"Yes. I'm preparing a little file about Devlin Associates, so that you'll have some background when you go north."

Good old Digby. The sudden intervention of the homicide people was not to be permitted to disturb the office routine.

"I'll be glad of anything you find," I confirmed, "I'm off to see a man now, but I should be with you in an hour or so."

The lightweight jacket, which I'd put on to cover up the gun I was carrying, had assumed all the characteristics of a three inch thick sheepskin as I picked my reluctant way through the parking lot. There was a heat shimmer dancing above the tops of the parked vehicles, and forming a hazy outline around the grim features of the cop who was standing by the car. The flap on his gun holster was unbuttoned, and his hand rested negligently two inches from the butt.

"Your name Preston?" he demanded.

"If it's about that tyre — " I began, but I knew it wasn't.

"Screw your tyre," he cut in, "There's people want to talk to you, down at headquarters. Let's go."

It was evident, from his tone and attitude, that he was in no mood for a debate. Having to tote all that equipment around in the heat of the day doesn't do anything for a man's temper. If I gave him an argument, he'd probably welcome the relief of bending that huge revolver over the back of my skull.

"Am I under arrest?"

"No way," he denied, "You're cooperating with the authorities, is all. Hand over the piece."

He held out one hand, and the other reduced the distance between fingers and gun-butt.

"What makes you think I'm carrying?"

The large face screwed up in derision.

"A joker," he scoffed, "Listen, anybody with a coat on a day like this, has to have something under it, right? Quit wasting my time."

I was very careful about the handover. He grunted, and stuck the weapon inside a voluminous shirt.

"O.K. you drive. I'll just tag on behind."

He waved a hand to indicate the gleaming Harley-Davidson propped against a concrete pillar. I nodded, and got inside my motorised sweat-box. The fan did its best, but all it did was to circulate the unbreathable air at a faster rate. Luckily, the drive was short, and soon I was locking up outside the ramshackle headquarters of the Monkton City P.D. My escort clumped along behind me, and stayed there until we reached the upper floor offices where Homicide was housed. Gil Randall was waiting on the landing, and I realised my cop-friend had been busy with his radio.

"You surrendered, then?" he greeted, with his usual heavy sarcasm.

"I can hardly breathe for laughing,"

I assured him, "Fine thing, when a citizen gets hauled in like some common criminal. I was on my way to see you."

"I'll bet." He looked at the khaki figure behind me, "Did he give you any trouble?"

"No sweat, serge," came the reply, "Tell you the truth, I wasn't in no mood for it. He had this on him."

He extended the thirty-eight, and Randall took it carefully, making the weapon look like a child's toy in his great fist.

"Thanks. We can handle this desperado now."

My companion clumped his way back down the stairs, and Randall motioned me through the familiar door of his inner sanctum. It is not an impressive room, scarcely large enough to house the two battered desks, and the row of grey file-cabinets which are the main furnishings. The window desk was vacant at the moment, which meant that I wasn't going to be subjected to the usual cross-fire between Randall and his superior. The big, sleepy looking sergeant was quite enough to cope with himself, and I was mildly relieved to find that the veteran Lieutenant Rourke was absent.

"Oh dear," I exclaimed, "I was hoping John would be here."

"I can imagine," he grunted, "But he has more important things to do than sit around gabbing it up with material witnesses."

I liked the description. It took me out of the premier league, which is reserved for suspects, accomplices before or after the fact of, and the like. Material witness, eh?

"Is that what I'm supposed to be? And just what is it I'm supposed to have witnessed materially?"

Randall lowered his enormous frame into the round-backed wooden chair behind his desk, and ignored the question.

"Have a seat," he offered.

I peeked at the chair first. They have a special one in that room, where one of the legs protrudes slightly through the seat. It isn't much of a protrusion, but it gets bigger and sharper the longer a man sits on it. After about half an hour of it, the average citizen is quite happy to confess to anything which will bring him relief. Today, the chair on offer was innocent of such little devices, so I parked.

"Go ahead," invited Randall.

"Go ahead and what?" I countered.

"Go ahead and tell me whatever it was you were coming here to tell me about."

Talking to Randall is always vaguely reminiscent of attending a first-year course in applied psychology. The interviewee is required to do all the work.

"I don't know why I was coming here," I told him smugly.

"Ah." He leaned the great head back, allowing four or five of his chins to stretch to an unaccustomed straight line, then dropped it again, so they could compress rapidly into their concertina comfort. "Let me help you. You came out of the Falcon Hotel, and thought to yourself, it's a fine sunny day, why don't I call in at headquarters, shoot a little breeze with a few old friends. Was that it?"

"No. Florence Digby had just told me

you wanted to see me, so I made it my first priority. As to why, I'm waiting."

"Ah yes, Miss Digby," he breathed approval, "Nice lady, very nice. Very efficient. She deserves better."

With which enigmatic pronouncement, he gave the chins another workout. I stared at the corner of the window, where an optimistic spider was slaving away at an intricate web, and wondered what he was hoping to trap. Any prey that wandered into that particular room was the exclusive property of Messrs. Rourke and Randall.

"Ever heard of Joseph Ralph?"

I hesitated. There are times for playing the innocent, and there are other times. Randall certainly knew something, or I wouldn't be sitting there. My wisest course was to try feeling him out, the same as he was doing to me.

"I've heard of him, yes."

"Good. We progress. Tell me about him."

I lit an Old Favourite, gaining valuable seconds in the process.

"I hear he's some kind of moneyman

in the tee-vee business. Finances new projects, that sort of thing. Out of my league, really."

"How well do you know him?" he asked casually.

"I don't know him at all," I rejected, "I never even laid eyes on the man. All I know is what I hear."

"From his wife, right? From Mrs. Ralph? Now, you wouldn't try to kid me she's out of your league? You two were pretty chummy, last I heard."

I put on a show of annoyance.

"What is this, a divorce preliminary? Mrs. Ralph is next thing to a total stranger. I scarcely know the lady."

"Maybe," he growled, all non-committal, "But you don't deny that you know her?"

"I've met her," I agreed, shortly.

"Tell me about it," he invited.

"Can't do that," I refused, "To do so would infringe on the confidentiality of an enquiry I'm working on."

One leg-of-beef hand passed slowly down the side of his face, making a rasping noise where the afternoon stubble was beginning to push through.

"The devil you can't. I asked you a question."

"And I answered you. I don't have to divulge information which has come to me in my professional capacity. Under the laws of the State of California — "

"The what? To hell with the laws of the State of California," he hissed nastily. "This here is my office you're in. I make the laws around here. If you want to spend the next forty-eight hours incommunicado, while you assist the department in the course of its official enquiries — in accordance with the laws of the State of California, naturally — then you go right ahead. I just don't have that kind of time to flim flam around. At the sound of the gong, it will be call-time."

His hand hovered over the bell-push on his desk, and I knew he meant business.

"I met her yesterday," I said quickly, "For the first time."

Reluctantly, he drew back the hand. I glanced upward, in momentary relief, to see that the spider had abandoned his project, and settled on the window-frame to watch an expert.

"What did you talk about?" he pressed, "And before you start giving me the runaround, I'll tell you something. I have a three-page statement, duly sworn and attested, which mentions your name three times. I know what Mrs. Ralph talked to you about. All I want from you is your side of it. Look," and he leaned forward, giving me all that man-to-man routine, which is even more dangerous to negotiate than straight-forward bullying, "There's no reason we should fight, Preston. I have all I need, right now. At a reasonable guess, I'd say you could be out of here in less than an hour. Quit being so defensive all the time, tell me what I want to know, and the door is behind you."

The spider was rubbing two of its legs together, which I took to be a form of applause. I could have learned to dislike the spider, but at the moment I was too busy with Randall. All this talk of sworn statements had a thoroughly unpleasant ring. The mere fact of Randall means homicide, and homicide means somebody bumped off somebody else, and the only thing I knew for certain was that my client was not the victim.

"She wanted me to take care of something for her," I told him.

"Don't be coy," he snapped, "What kind of something?"

"There was a man making a nuisance of himself. Mrs. Ralph didn't want her husband to find out, so she asked me if I could talk to the man."

Even as I said it, I could hear it clanging emptily in that stuffy room, and the impatient disbelief in Randall's eyes did not waver.

"What way was he being a nuisance?"

"He'd made up some yarn about having an affair with her."

The vast creases above his eyebrows rolled around like thunderclouds.

"Get to the blackmail," he urged, "How much did he want?"

"Twenty-five thousand," I admitted reluctantly.

"Good. Good. That ties in with my information. It'll get easier now you've started. Tell me the rest."

I told him most of it, leaving out any reference to the stolen bills, and keeping my fingers crossed. The main storyline was old as the hills, and wouldn't cause many raised eyebrows in my present surroundings. The money was a different position entirely. I wasn't protecting anyone else by not mentioning it. Not Ellen Ralph, not Joe Ralph, not anybody but Preston M., licensed investigator, of this parish. Nobody was going to mind me doing my stuff on a straightforward blackmail case, but the money would change all that. Stolen cash, which has crossed a state line is a federal matter, and my feet wouldn't touch the ground if the lawmen knew I suppressed that kind of knowledge.

When I finished my yarn, leaving out my latest interview with Ellen Ralph, and making no reference to the man Shapiro, there was a silence for a few moments. Then Randall asked softly:

"And where do I find Mrs. Ralph now?"

"I don't know," I shrugged, "Like I

told you, the last I heard from her was this telephone call. She said her husband had forced the story out of her, and she'd been so afraid she'd run away."

He squinted at me ferociously, uncertain whether I was holding out on him. Finally, he said:

"Well, it seems to check out. If it was anybody else but you, I'd wrap this up and put it away. The trouble is, it's all too simple, too straightforward. With you around, I like to find problems. Straight down the line is not your ballgame, Preston. There always has to be an angle, something devious."

He was fishing now, and I had a rush of confidence.

"Nice talk," I said huffily, "Here I come walking into headquarters, of my own free will — "

" — Under armed escort, — " he interpolated.

" — I was coming anyway," I objected, "I come in here, make a full statement — "

" — Full — "

" — And all I get is insults. Come on

Gil, I've told you all I know. Why don't you tell me what's going down? What's with all these sworn statements?"

He hesitated, but more out of habit than wish. Randall was in the business of gathering information, not parting with it.

"Well, what the hell," he shrugged, "It'll be on the news anyway. No harm in telling you what everybody in town will know one hour from now. Mr. Joseph Ralph, your snow-white client's old man, took a gun to one Harold Mason today, and blew three holes in him. The said Mason is now the late Mason, and the said Ralph is locked up downstairs. It was him gave me the statement, with your name on it. I don't like any of it."

Even allowing for his nature, which was automatically one of dark suspicion, I couldn't see his point.

"Come on, Gil, what's the mystery? Oldest story in the world. Man finds out his wife is playing around, and he blows up the opposition. Even the jury won't blame him. Ralph will cop three to five, and be out in two years. Why do you have to make everything so difficult?"

Apart from my own relief at having been able to avoid the pitfalls of the marked money, I was genuinely puzzled by Randall's unwillingness to accept the old triangle situation.

"It goes against the grain," he told me reluctantly, "But I'm beginning to think you really don't know."

"What don't I really know?"

"Ralph, Mr. Ralph, husband of your Mrs. Ralph. You really don't know who he is, do you?"

I shrugged.

"Why would I? Movie finance, that's a closed area to me. You'd have to be in the business to understand the way those things work. Are you saying it's crooked?"

"O.K."

He brought a giant hand down on the desk top, and dust particles leaped off everything in sight. Even the spider retreated anxiously into a corner. There was no cause for alarm. The handslap was merely a signal that Randall had made up his mind about something.

"I've decided to believe you, and the reason I've decided is because I think you have a fine concern for your own health. You're not always as smart as you imagine, Preston, but when it comes to self-protection you're a whizz. If you knew what I know, when all this started, you'd have thanked the lady very kindly for thinking of you, and caught the next plane to Alaska."

"Why? I've handled dozens of cases exactly like this."

I didn't like his tone, and I didn't at all care for the implication that my health might suffer.

"Not exactly like it. Not exactly. You see, Mr. Ralph is not quite what Mrs. Ralph thinks he is. In fact, he wasn't Mr. Ralph at all, until about five years ago. Did you ever hear tell of the Ralfini family of Detroit?"

If I'd been apprehensive before, I was beginning to feel positively jittery now. The Ralfini's are one of the big families in the nationwide crime syndicate, and had received their due share of publicity during the recent hearings.

"I'm beginning to like this," I said.

"It gets worse," he assured me blandly, "Your friend Ralph, formerly Ralfini, used to be an active member in that city, but he always had problems controlling his temper. If he'd been anybody else, they'd have made a traffic diversion out of him, but as he was a close blood relative, they gave him one last chance. They sent him out here with a new name, told him to watch his temper, and it was the end of the road. I guess they must have scared the hell out of him, because he certainly played in a low key all the time he's been here. But, he couldn't take this stuff about his wife, and he reacted exactly the way he would have in the old days. He smoked out lover-boy, from where you had him stashed away, and put the blast on him. Nothing subtle about your Mr. Ralph. Broad daylight, public place. He must've been out of his head."

"That's what the lawyers will claim," I replied automatically, "And don't call him my Mr. Ralph."

But my mind was elsewhere. Family

people are very conservative, very tidy-minded. They were going to be mad with Joe for doing what he did, but he would not be their main concern. That would be with the money, their money, which Joe Ralph was supposed to take care of. As for Randall's crack that the man was out of his head, it was significant that there had been no reference to the stolen bills. Joe hadn't been that far off-balance, because if he had, there wouldn't have been any question of my walking out of headquarters. Randall, within the limits of his profession, is something of a friend of mine, but there is no way he would let me get away with a stunt like that. In any case, if it was in the statement, it would be out of his hands.

No, so far as the law was concerned, I probably had a clean bill. Well, cleanish.

Not so the family.

Joe Ralph would stick to his outraged husband routine, for the benefit of the police and the eventual trial. But he would tell the family the whole tale, and they would be wanting to talk to me, that much was certain. Whatever else they might want to do to me was not so certain, and I didn't care to dwell on it.

Randall was as good as his word. Thirty minutes, and two typed pages of statement later, I was back out on the street. It's a wonderful thing, to be a free man, in a free society.

As I drove out of the parking lot, I was already starting to make frequent checks to see if I could spot anyone on my tail.

The Ralfini's, I knew, would have little time for the democratic process.

9

It was four-thirty when I got into the office, and Florence Digby was waiting to pounce.

"Not right away, Florence," I hedged, "There is one phone call I have to make, then I'm at your service."

With the door firmly closed, I put through a call to the Falcon Hotel, and asked for Six-O-Five. Sam Thompson's careful voice said:

"Six-O-Five."

"It's me, Sam. Let me talk to the lady."

When she came on the line, I told her what happened, and that her husband was locked up. She almost cried with relief, and must have been even more afraid of the man than I'd realised.

"You think it's safe for me to go home?" she queried, "You don't suppose those so-called detectives will be there, do you?"

I'd forgotten the bodyguards, in all the excitement.

"I doubt it, but it might be wise not to take any chances. Tell you what I suggest. Watch the television until there's a newscast. The story has to break very soon. Once you see it, get in touch with the police, tell them you've been hiding from your husband, but that you'll meet them at the house. If those characters are still there, you'll come to no harm with the law around. I don't see why they should bother you, anyway. They're strictly employees, and with your husband locked up, they don't have a part to play."

Even as I said that, I wondered about the truth of it. But Ellen Ralph couldn't spend the rest of her life hiding in hotel rooms. Whatever it was she had to face, the sooner it happened the better. There was one vital area to be covered first.

"When you talk to the police, Mrs. Ralph," I impressed on her, "Don't go into any details about the money. You know nothing about it. All you know is, your husband is in the habit of keeping large sums in the house, and you don't have any ideas about where it came from, or what he does with it."

She thought about it, then said, "Why not? After all, if Joe's committed murder, surely no one is going to worry about income tax evasion?"

But I had anticipated that objection.

"By him, no," I agreed, "They could still charge you as being a knowing accessory, and that carries heavy penalties. It goes beyond that, too. If the police know about the money, they'll want to know where it came from, and that will not please the people who supply it. You're going to have to take my word for this, Mrs. Ralph, but some of those people are not the straight forward business characters your husband would have you believe. They are going to get very upset if the law starts poking around, and you will not be one of their favourite people. Do you understand what I'm saying?"

"You think I could be in some danger from these people?" she asked tremulously.

"I'm saying it's a distinct possibility, yes," I confirmed. "Take my advice, and just be the innocent housewife. Any other way, you'll just bring trouble, for me as well as yourself. And it could be very big trouble."

I made my tone as hard as I could. It was vital that Ellen Ralph should avoid any complications. Once the story hit the street, she would have her hands full, as it was. The media were going to have a field day with a good old-fashioned lurid love-triangle. Not to mention the extra added ingredients. She was herself a former tee-vee favourite, for one thing, and her husband had known Mafia connections. The dead man, Harry Mason, might only have been a casino dealer in life, but in death he would become a prominent and notorious Palm Springs gambler.

The next few weeks were going to be busy and unpleasant for my client, and it would have taken more than an act of Congress to prevent it. The fact hadn't dawned on her yet, and she seemed to be deluding herself that now Joe had done what he'd done, the matter was ended. Well, it was no part of my job to disillusion her about that. My concern was with a little matter of hot money, the Ralfini family of Detroit, and the personal health and welfare of one Preston M.

After a few more exchanges, during which I hammered home the point time and again, I asked her to let Sam Thompson go, once she checked out of the hotel. Then I put down the phone, and sat there, frowning at the walls.

Was there something else I could be doing? Anything at all, which would give me a clean bill with the Ralfini's? It's an odd reflection on the realities of existence, that I was far more concerned about putting one foot wrong with those people than I was with the police.

La Digby poked her head around the door.

"Could we deal with these things now?"

I waved her inside. There is something oddly calming about that lady. Her correct, formal attire, and her correct formal attitude to the world have to represent something. A place where bills get paid, trains run on time, and the guy in the white hat always wins in the end. Maybe there is such a place, for all I know, but it had contrived to elude me for all these many years. Anyway, here she was again, all notebooked and pencilled up, arranging the immaculate skirt neatly over the attractive knees.

"First of all," she reported primly, "We can forget about Mr. Schwarzenkopf."

"Mr. Who?"

Without exactly sighing with exasperation, she managed to look as though she had done just that.

"Elias Schwarzenkopf, the man who ran away with the payroll and the underage office junior," she reminded.

"Oh, that one." Pity, I'd been half-hoping old Elias would be the statistic that got away. "They nabbed him, eh?"

"Well — er — not exactly. He — er — that is Mr. Schwarzenkopf is now deceased."

For some unaccountable reason, Miss Digby seemed to be colouring up in the cheek area.

"You surprised me," I admitted, "I

wouldn't have thought old Elias was shoot-out material. Just goes to show, you never can tell."

"It wasn't like that," she corrected, "It seems that he had a weak heart, and that was what he died from. In a motel over at Santa Monica."

She seemed anxious to move on to the next subject, but I had this feeling I wasn't getting the entire scam on Schwarzenkopf. A heart attack. And a motel? Suddenly, I put in the rest of the story.

"Where was Lolita when this happened?" I asked her.

"Close by, I understand. Very close, I believe."

The pink in her cheeks was now working its way into the dusky reds, and I knew my assumption had been correct.

"That close, huh? Well, they say it's the only way to go. I'll bet, if Schwarzenkopf had been given a list of available alternatives, that's the one he'd have gone for."

As it was, he'd been better off than

Harry Mason, I reflected. Florence Digby was beginning to look as if she'd be grateful if the floor was to open up, and swallow her.

"O.K. Scratch Schwarzenkopf." It was time to end the ribbing. "What else have you got?"

She was so relieved at the change of subject, that she almost galloped over the next few words.

"I've learned a little more about Devlin Associates. They seem to be very reputable people indeed. I've typed out a little history for you. It will fit into your pocket, if you wanted to read it on the plane."

I took the papers from her, and riffled at them quickly. She was right. There'd be enough there to keep my mind off the air bumps. About to place it on one side, I changed my mind, glancing over the names of the directors. I couldn't have said what prompted me to do that, unless it was idle curiosity, but I knew what brought me back to the present with a jolt. Halfway down the list a name almost leapt off the page.

Leonard Shapiro.

Coincidence? Anything is possible in this world, but I didn't buy that. The man I'd seen leaving Harry Mason's rented bungalow at Fisherman's Quay had been Leonard Shapiro. For some reason, Mason had told me his name was Arthur Arthurson, but I'd already established that Arthurson was long dead. Either Mason had told me a lie, for reasons which I'd probably never know, or else he really believed Shapiro was Arthurson.

That was point one.

Point two was that I'd received what sounded like a nice routine commission from Devlin Associates, the very day that Harry Mason got himself killed, although I hadn't known at the time. And here was that name again, the selfsame Shapiro, cropping up in this seemingly unrelated quarter.

I have nothing against the name. Some of my best friends are Leonard Shapiros, but these two (or was it one?) did not appear on that list. A man with a nasty suspicious turn of mind might think things, and I happen to be a man with a nasty S.T. of M.

Until that moment, I'd been undecided as to what I could do that might be of some use in the Ralph case. Now, I hadn't any doubt.

"Florence, you're beautiful."

I beamed at her, but she'd had too much experience of me to let that get her excited.

"Just routine, Mr. Preston," she replied primly, "Do you want me to arrange for your flight this evening?"

I tapped exultantly at the papers in my hand.

"Nope. Some sixth sense tells me I might not be going. Not right away, that is." Then seeing the familiar disapproval clouds beginning to gather, as she diagnosed work-evasion, I hurried on, "Sergeant Randall wouldn't want me to leave town right at this moment. I'm kind of helping the department."

"Oh?"

With some people an oh is just an oh. The delectable Digby can pack into it an entire interrogation, plus a strong element of suspicion, with more than a hint of hurt pride. Well, she could get on with it. The Ralph case had not really come to much of anything, certainly not enough to justify one of her famous files. Such money as might have come my way, and which I might have regarded as a kind of tax-free bonus, had immediately floated out on the next tide. Now that the caper had been brought to an abrupt conclusion, there was no point in all that office routine of hers. As a conscience salver. I also told myself that what she didn't know couldn't hurt her.

"Shouldn't take long," I said breezily, "The whole thing should be over and done with by tomorrow. Next day at the latest. I'll explain to Mr. Devlin, and thank you for the rundown."

I made it a dismissal and she went away, dissatisfied. When the door was closed, I looked up the number of the realty company again, the one founded by the late Arthur Arthurson, and put in a call.

"Mr. Shapiro, please."

"Mr. Shapiro?" The girl sounded

slightly puzzled. Then she said, "Just hold the line please." She must have conferred with someone else in the office, because when she finally came back on the line she said, "Mr. Shapiro is not due at the office today. He is one of the directors of the company, and doesn't actually have a desk here. I'm sure someone else could help you — "

" — No. It's a personal matter," I interrupted, "I'll call him at home. Thanks for your trouble."

Leonard Shapiro was beginning to be a very interesting man. He was a director of Devlin Associates, which found assignments for worthy investigators in far-off places. He was also a director of a realty firm, which accommodated itinerant blackmailers on their way through the city. To round it off, he was some kind of associate of Joe Ralph, née Ralfini, lately of Detroit, who was in the surplus currency business. If I'd had any sense, I'd have called Gil Randall, and told him about this fascinating character. The reason I didn't do that was simple. One way and another, I was fourteen hundred plus dollars out of pocket, as a result of all these goings on, and it seemed to me somebody should make up the deficit. In addition to that, if Mr. Shapiro turned out to be what I thought he might, some kind of outrider for the national syndicate, then it was important for those people to know I was just an innocent bystander.

I dug out the small list of Shapiros I'd already called from the directory. Only two of them admitted outright to the 'Leonard', the others hiding coyly behind the initial 'L'. It never pays to overlook the obvious, as I started on with the first Leonard. From the guarded tones of the woman who answered, I thought I might have got a bullseye with the first shot. It took several questions and evasions before I finally learned that Leonard Shapiro was safely tucked away in a rest home, where he'd been resting for the past six years.

The second call was answered by a man with an open cheery kind of delivery.

"Speaking."

"My name is Griffiths," I told him. That was the name under which Harry

Mason had been operating, when he rented the beach bungalow at Fisherman's Quay. If I had the right man, he would recognise the name. If I hadn't, it was a small enough deception, "I got your number from Devlin Associates."

"The Devlin you did," he quipped, "Well I'm going to have to reprimand somebody about that. Griffiths, you say? I don't believe I know you, Mr. Griffiths."

There was nothing evasive about this Shapiro. He was all up-front, let's put our cards on the table, and why don't we all talk frankly about this. A genuine, twentieth century glad-handler, and no doubt with an income to match. The trouble with those people is, they can talk for an hour without saying anything. And I wanted him to say something.

"We haven't met," I replied, "But you know my brother, Harry, You rented him a bungalow down on the seafront. I'd like to talk with you, Mr. Shapiro, and not on the phone."

He let me wait for a moment, while he chewed on it.

"A bungalow, you say? Well, tell you

the truth, Mr. Griffiths, I don't have a lot to do with the daily running of things. Still, if you want to talk, that's fine with me. Always open for business, twenty-four hours a day. I'm kind of tied up at the moment, but I could probably fit you in later this evening. Care to give me some idea of what it's all about? No complaints about the beach house, I trust?"

That was the real estate man in him coming out. Any ramshackle hut with a new paint job became elevated automatically to beach house status. To do the man justice, I had to remember that there could be other people listening at his end, people who never heard of Harry Mason or Joe Ralph.

"Not that I know of," I denied, "I'm with an audience research unit. There's talk of re-running some of the old television shows, and we'd appreciate your views. We're especially interested in 'That Girl Susie'. Like to know what you feel about it."

That was the title of Ellen Ralph's

old programme, in the days when she'd been Ellen Brady. The mention of it should be sufficient notice that things were indeed up front, cards on the table, and we should by all means talk frankly.

"Hmm," he mused, "Well that sort of thing can take a little time, I imagine. Could we make it a semi-social meeting, do you think? I'm due out at the Foxtrot Inn tonight. You know where that is?"

I knew it. A new place, out in the desert on Highway Ten.

"I can find it," I confirmed, "What time?"

"Around nine o'clock? Fine, fine. Just tell Robert, the M.D. when you arrive. I'll have him watch out for you. What's your full name, Mr. Griffiths? You must call me Leonard, by the way."

"Fine with me, Leonard. The full name is Mark Preston Griffiths, without the Griffiths."

Some of the spontaneous joy was missing from his voice when he'd absorbed that.

"Ah yes, I was beginning to wonder

whether it might be. Nine o'clock then?"

If this tone was anything to judge by, he had plenty to think about when he broke the connection.

So had I.

10

When I said the Foxtrot Inn was a new place, I wouldn't want to be misunderstood. I didn't intend to give the impression that there was anything new about the building itself. Only the name's new, and no doubt the decor, which I hadn't yet seen. The place itself was built some time around the turn of the century, when the city fathers took it into their heads to clean up the 'festering cesspit of our tenderloin district, a badge of shame for all decent citizens', as one newsleader read at the time. The city fathers, being men of a practical turn of mind, were at the same time reluctant to see all that easy money stray too far from home. What they did was to transport the saloons, the tables and the girls, especially the girls, outside the city limits, and to scatter them around so that they wouldn't be faced with a transplanted tenderloin in a few years time. One such establishment had been the place I was now heading for, and it had undergone many changes of owner since those days. During the prohibition years it had suffered revisions in the management structure faster than a mortician could count, often to the accompaniment of the sub-machine gun. In World War Two it went through its patriotic phase, providing much needed relaxation for the highly paid aircraft workers, and the fresh-faced refugees from nearby boot camps. At a price, naturally.

Since then, the fortunes of the place had waxed and waned, in a pattern roughly comparable to the movements of the local economy, but it never actually failed. No matter how tough things are in the world, the places with the bright lights are usually the last to suffer.

In the previous five years there had been the Funky Goat, The Country 'n' Bestern (ouch) and the Desert Paradise. Now we had the Foxtrot Inn, and I made a left off Ten, to negotiate the two-car wide concrete ribbon leading down to the club.

It was almost dark now, and a bunch of motor-cyclists at the side of the road were using flashlights as they repaired a machine which lay forlornly on its side. I couldn't be certain whether they'd already visited the Foxtrot, or were on their way in when they had the blowout or whatever. Not that it mattered very much, in their timescale, because their story would be very brief either way. The out-of-town dine and dance joints don't exactly cater for juvenile hell-raisers, and usually know how to deal with them.

Business seemed to be slow tonight. There was room for a hundred cars at least out front, but there were plenty of wide open spaces, and I left plenty of room either side as I parked. As I locked up, I could already appreciate the lower temperature out there. After the furnace of the city any drop in the gauge came as a boon, and my step was almost springy as I made my way over to the entrance.

Everything seemed to be black and white, which I imagined was some kind of attempt at a period atmosphere. The foxtrot was a type of dance back in the twenties, but I hadn't been aware that it carried its own colour scheme. Inside, a couple of muscular characters in tuxedos gave me a friendly nod as I went through, but they didn't fool me. They could just as quickly dispense the old heave-ho if anybody tried to disturb the routine, which was the painless transfer of cash from the clientele, into the safe-keeping of the owners.

"Is Robert around?" I asked vaguely, of no one in particular.

A small dark man materialised in front of me, looking for all the world like a refugee from a Central American revolution.

"I am Robert, sir. Can I be of assistance?"

He didn't say Robert, he said Rowbear, and he also said asseestance. The greasy black hair with the centre parting was all part of the foxtrot act, but the general effect was to make me promise myself not to turn my back on him.

"I'm meeting a friend, a Mr. Shapiro?"

"Oh yes. Pleese to follow me."

I pleesed to follow him, through a

small bar where a few people sipped at highly-coloured drinks full of salad. A girl with long black hair was draped across the bar, and she looked up hopefully as we entered. I pulled my shoulders back automatically but I needn't have bothered. She looked at me, then through me, and finally resumed her inspection of the counter. The part-time assassin half-turned, to ensure I was still behind him, as we went into the large dining area. The black and white had really been developed in there, where the walls were in a check pattern, making them for all the world like king-size crossword puzzles. The table covers alternated between all black and all white, and the tiny dance-floor was of gleaming ebony. Even the band was a mixture, with white and black faces alternating on the shiny white platform. Whether that was a result of management policy of a simple demonstration in the breakdown of cultural barriers I really wouldn't know, but a sociologist could spend happy hours theorising about it. Nobody had to theorise about the music, which was a faithful rooty toot resurrection of old-fashioned arrangements, right down to the vocalist with the megaphone. There was only one couple dancing, a fat fifty year old man sweating and cavorting, more or less in time with the beat, while a languid twenty year old girl with a fixed smile pretended to join in.

Diners were scattered thinly around, watched by bored waiters in butterfly collars and period dinner jackets. If the present evidence was anything to judge by, it wouldn't be too long before the Foxtrot Inn followed the Desert Paradise and other previous occupants into oblivion. In the far corner of the room, and secluded by some black and white trellis work, four private booths held pride of place. Robert led me to the second of these, waving me inside with a half-bow.

A man sat there, watching my arrival from hooded brown eyes.

"Right on time," he greeted, "Have a seat."

He made no effort to get up, and the well-tended hands remained resting on the black table-cloth. We had a look at each other while I was settling into the white wooden chair. Leonard Shapiro was pushing forty, and he'd spent a lot of that time living soft. What should have been a sharp jawline was obscured by surplus flesh, and the mouth beneath the Wyatt Earp moustache was puffy. If the creases were to be believed, my host spent a lot of time smiling, and his whole expression suggested a life-style of genial self-indulgence. Well, when I say his whole expression, that doesn't include the eyes, which retained an independent watchfulness. The presentation was topped off by a luxuriant head of jet-black curly hair, greying slightly at the temples. When he spoke, his accent was more east coast than west.

"You don't seem to be a very safe man to know. I heard on the news about Mr. Mason. A terrible thing."

"Terrible," I agreed drily, "But it had nothing to do with me. They have the man who did that."

"Ah yes," he shrugged expensive

shoulders, "But they didn't say how Mr. Mason was traced. That address at Fisherman's Quay was supposed to be confidential. Mason even used this other name Griffiths, so that he could have a little privacy. Now, it seems to me that somebody had to tell Joe Ralph where he was, and I certainly was not responsible. Who do you think it could have been?"

Fortunately, I used to play a lot of poker, so surprises don't always register on my face. From the way he spoke, Shapiro hadn't been aware that I'd moved Mason out of Fisherman's Quay, and that Joe Ralph had traced him to the beach hut. That would have to mean that Ellen hadn't told him about the move, which in turn could mean that he wasn't as involved in the killing as I'd suspected. Not that he was off the list, by a longchalk. All the same, I was puzzled.

"If you're looking at me, forget it," I advised, "I never even laid eyes on Ralph. You're the one he was chummy with."

"Me?" Some of the creases around his

eyes deepened, “I think ‘chummy’ is a little strong. I’ve had dealings with the man, but we’re not exactly in each other’s pockets. You, on the other hand, had information he might pay for. A dollar is a dollar, and I don’t imagine you’re too fussy about where you pick one up.”

The tone was light but the eyes were cold, and I was sorely tempted to reach out and plant a fist in one of them. But this was not the time to be tossing out my cool.

“Sticks and stones, fat man,” I replied evenly, “What was this information I was supposed to sell your old buddy?”

He didn’t like the crack about his weight, but evidently decided I wasn’t to be the only one who knew how to hang on to his temper.

“I would have thought that was obvious,” he said stiffly, “You knew where the boyfriend was hiding. Plenty of husbands would pay to know that, and Joe could certainly afford it. It would hardly have been Ellen, would it, and nobody else knew.”

I lit an Old Favourite, thinking.

"Look we're not going to get anywhere, sitting here making cracks at each other. When Ellen Ralph came to you, looking for a place where Mason could stay, what story did she tell you?"

He stared at me hard before replying. Then he shrugged.

"I guess there's no harm in your knowing that. She told me Mason was a relative, and that her husband hated him. Some old family row, she said. Mason was hiding from his own wife, some big alimony settlement, and was getting out of the country. All he wanted was somewhere to stay for a few days, while he cashed up his assets, and could I find him a place that was cheap and quiet. He couldn't use his own name, because his wife's lawyers were trying to trace him. It seemed a small enough favour to me, and I helped the lady out. She's not an easy one to turn down, once she turns to those baby blues, or hadn't you noticed?"

It sounded plausible enough, and I nodded slowly.

"I'd noticed. So, the next thing you

knew was when you heard about the murder?"

"Right." He rested his immaculate sleeves on the table, and lowered his voice, "Now it's your turn. How did you come to put me in this picture?"

"Easy," I answered, without hesitating, "I saw you there, down at the quay."

"Saw me? When?"

"Last night. I went to see Mason, and you were just leaving."

Pudgy fingers drummed soundlessly on the heavy cloth.

"You recognised me? I would have hoped I wasn't that well known."

"Never saw you before," I assured him, "But you had a car, cars have plates, and plates can be traced."

"You went to all that trouble? You're a very thorough person."

"When I sit down at a table, I like to know who else is playing," I replied.

"Fair enough, but if you're on the level, and I say 'if', why didn't you tell the police about me? I'm sure you didn't, or they'd have been in touch hours ago."

I flicked ash into a black glass ashtray.

"I'm not paid to do their work. Let them find their own Shapiros. The way things are, I doubt whether they'll ever find out that Harry Mason even spoke to you."

"So you kept me out of it," he said softly, almost as though he was speaking to himself, "Not that I'm in it, not really, but I prefer to keep a low profile, and this kind of thing never does anybody any good. I guess I owe you one. So why are you here?"

"Just tidying up loose ends."

"What's loose?" he queried, "Ellen Ralph tried to hide her boyfriend away. Her husband found out about it, and killed him. The police have the man locked up, and that is the end of that. A nasty little story, but commonplace enough. I don't see why you're still sniffing around."

Threats come in all shapes and sizes, but never in a form that I can't recognise. Leonard Shapiro's air of puzzled enquiry didn't fool me. I've been warned off by experts, and I can always tell. What I didn't know was why, and I never have learned when to leave well enough alone.

"Well, I'll level with you," I announced breezily, and with no such intention, "The fact is, nobody paid me yet, and so far I am fourteen hundred dollars out of pocket. Getting paid for what I do is a very sensitive area with me. As you say, the police have old Joe locked up, and that's very nice for them, but it doesn't buy me any groceries. What's motivating me is the old profit column, and I'm going to carry on sniffing around, as you put it, until I come out in front. You can understand that, I imagine?"

"Ah." He sat back in the chair, as though pleased with what he'd heard. People are all the same. You can talk to them about honour, or principles, or ideals, until you're blue in the face, and they just don't get it, not at any gut-level. But once you wave aloft the good green dollar, they are with you all the way. It gives them a firm ground to stand on, a position from which to negotiate. Shapiro was now on familiar territory, "Let's see, you've been involved in this one day, a day and a half? You price yourself pretty high, don't you?"

"That doesn't include pain and suffering," I told him blandly, "Let me break it down for you. Ellen Ralph paid me one thousand dollars advance, expenses to be extra. I paid out some expenses, and I had a few dollars of my own already in my fold. Some of Joe Ralph's heavies beat me over the head, and took it all away. Total, fourteen hundred. I want it back."

I made no reference to my little attempt to pay off Big Jule Keppler. For one thing, I didn't want him involved at any level, and for another, it never pays to show all your cards at the same time. That only happens when you're called, and we hadn't reached that point yet. Shapiro listened intently while I talked, then looked astonished, "Am I hearing you right? Did you say 'heavies'? You make Ralph sound like some kind of hoodlum, instead of a respectable business man. If you say you were robbed, well, maybe you were, but I think you're stretching your imagination a little by blaming it on Ralph."

But he didn't take the high tone that might have been expected from one legitimate citizen defending another. I felt he was inviting me to say a little more, so I did.

"Not my imagination," I denied, "The imagination belongs to a big slob named Randall. He's a sergeant out of homicide, and he imagines all kinds of stuff about Ralph, right back to his old days in Detroit."

His features became very bland.

"Detroit?"

"That's what Randall says, and he's usually very careful with his words. Personally, I'm not very interested. I don't stick my nose in things that don't concern me. What concerns me is the fourteen hundred. I'd like to take it up with Joe Ralph, but the way things are, that's out."

"Yes, I see. What I don't see is what any of this has got to do with me. Don't get me wrong," and he made a deprecatory move with his hands, "Nice talking to you and all that, but you still haven't said why you wanted to see me."

It was my turn to look astonished.

"Did I forget to mention that? I wondered why you wanted me out of town."

I sat back, all honest-faced, and waited for his response. To do him credit, he scarcely faltered.

"You go too fast for me," he said slowly, "What makes you think I want you out of town?"

"Two and two, the old arithmetic. You're mixed up with Ellen Ralph, Joe Ralph, Harry Mason. Ralph kills Mason, and a few hours later you offer me a job at the other end of the state. Why?"

"I offered you a job?" he began, "I don't — "

"Oh cut it out," I interrupted, "We're too old for this kind of stuff. Devlin Associates is what I'm talking about. You're on the board, and that makes it your offer. All I'm asking is, why? What is it I might find out if I stick around?"

He made a deep, sighing sound, and

looked me straight in the face.

"If you took the trouble to ask around, you would find I am on the board of seventeen companies and corporations in this immediate area. How they conduct their daily business is none of my concern, and I don't intend to make it my concern. Right now, I think you've wasted quite enough of my time. I'm obliged to you for not involving me with the police over this nasty business, but I don't think that's worth fourteen hundred dollars. I'm just an ordinary legitimate business man, and I don't want any further part of the Ralph case, or of you. As for Devlin, he's a sound man. If he has a job for you, I'd recommend that you take it, but that's for you to decide. I bid you goodnight."

Since he showed no sign of getting up, and it was his table, that made it my move. There had probably been times in my life when I made less progress, but offhand I couldn't recall one. I got up, trying to look inscrutable.

"Too bad we couldn't get together. Maybe next time."

"There'll be no next time," he dismissed, "And don't come here again."

"It's a public place," I paused in mid-sentence, "Don't tell me, you're on the board, right?"

"Correct."

Rowbear materialised from the black and white decor, and escorted me as far as the door.

"Nice place," I told him, "Friendly atmosphere."

"Glad you enjoyed your veeseet, Mr. Preston."

So he knew all the time. I went thoughtfully down the steps, sending the cigarette butt in a curving arc into the night air. The moon was on full parade now, an enormous yellow orb spreading out its milky light all over the desert, and bringing a touch of mystery to the half-seen hills in the distance. As I walked towards the parking lot, I thought I saw movement. Another few yards, and I could identify figures, prowling around. It looked like a couple of the motorcycle kids I'd noticed on the way in, and whatever they were doing, it was bad news for somebody. They seemed to be moving from one car to the next, probably spraying paint remover or worse. Whatever it was, they were now almost level with my own heap, which galvanised me into sudden activity.

"Hey," I yelled, running between the fence posts and waving my fists.

A startled blur of white faces turned towards me, and somebody shouted with alarm. They ducked down out of view, and a car door slammed. My car door. Roaring obscenities and threats I moved as fast as I could, but I knew I'd never make the distance before they got away. A starter motor whirred in the stillness, and I was still twenty yards short of the goal. Suddenly, the car leaped forwards. There was an almighty explosion, and I seemed to be in the middle of some slow-motion disaster movie.

The car became the epi-centre of a holocaust, a deep red obscenity of mushrooming fire, turning to orange as it grew, then yellow at the edges. A great ball of black smoke plumed upwards, obscuring the hanging moon.

My feet left the ground as strong winds grabbed me up tossing me around and around like a rag doll. Something loomed up ahead of me, and I threw up instinctive hands to protect my face, knowing at the same time that it was hopeless.

There was one instant of total clarity, a bitter resentment that this was a hell of a way to go. Then I smashed headlong into something, and took no further interest.

11

Somewhere, on the other side of my aching eyelids, there was light, but I wasn't ready for it yet. First I had to get some semblance of order inside the foggy soup which was my mind. Something about the night, I recalled, and the car. Yes, that was it. It was night-time and I'd been heading towards the car. For some reason, the car decided to blow up. Why would it do that, I wondered? Well, no matter. It was all in the past now. I was dead, and would have to adjust to this new environment, but not until I was good and ready. That light meant that a whole experience was waiting, and there were odds to be calculated.

I had some vague childhood images to draw on, and as best I could remember, there were two possibilities. This new environment would be controlled either by little red men with horns and pitchforks, or by serene beings with harps and wings. Given the choice, I was a harp and wing man every time, but I seemed to recall the whole decision was based on some kind of score sheet. If that was true, there was little doubt the other team would have a distinct edge. Well, I wasn't licked yet. There was probably an angle somewhere, and if there was, I would find it.

Wondering what kind of shape I'd arrived in, I squirmed around. There was a dull ache here, and another one there, but no bones seemed to be broken. I squiggled my fingers gratefully, and they all responded. A final deep breath, and I raised a red eyelid. I seemed to be in some kind of clearing house, probably waiting my turn for a decision. Everything was white and restful, and I would have been quite happy to stay where I was.

The light was obscured suddenly and a grave face hovered above me, cool grey eyes inspecting me with concern. I couldn't see the wings from that position, but I know an angel when I see one, and all in white, too. She smelled cool and fragrant, like an early morning stream, and I smiled thankfully.

"Don't try to talk, Mr. Clancy," she advised quietly. "The doctor will be with you directly."

Mr. Who? And what was all this talk about doctors? The angel didn't seem to know much about her business. Maybe she was new. As for Mr. Clancy, whoever he might be, he had his nerve, trying to pass himself off as me. The face went away, and I tried to sit up, but a gentle hand restrained me.

I lay back, unresisting, while what would have been about five earth minutes ticked away. Then a new face appeared, but this one had a bandit moustache and a collar and tie. That was when I had my first suspicion that I might not be quite as dead as I'd imagined.

"Well, Mr. Clancy, you've certainly had a good rest," greeted the bandit.

It was time for a few forceful questions, I decided.

"Wh — wh — ?" I squawked.

"Just take it easy," he advised. "You're had a very close shave Mr. Clancy, and you're lucky to be alive. But there's nothing broken. You have a few bruises, but they'll soon clear up. I don't see why you shouldn't be able to leave tomorrow. You've been unconscious for thirty-six hours, and your body will have made good use of the time. Nurse Rogers will stay with you, and I'll call in later."

I managed a nod and he went away. Then I closed my eyes as though drifting off to sleep, but in reality I needed some thinking time. A man who suddenly finds he isn't dead has some adjusting to do. This business with the name, now, that was a puzzler. I carry enough identification for three ordinary people, what with my badge and my — no I don't. I suddenly recalled that when I changed jackets, before leaving for the Foxtrot Inn, I deliberately left the wallet behind, pushing a few loose bills into my pocket for expenses. The hospital staff would naturally search me for identity clues, but why Clancy? I didn't even know anybody — yes, I did. There'd been a man call at the office a couple of weeks earlier, wanting to sell me an encyclopedia of crime. He'd been a hard man to get rid of, and I'd finally taken his card, shoving it in a pocket. That was all they'd been able to find, so now I was Clancy.

I ran through it again. If I was Clancy, and Clancy had been asleep for thirty-six hours, that meant I'd missed out entirely on Wednesday. This must be Thursday morning, and the world outside had been short of one Preston, M. for all that time. It was all too much to deal with, and I must have fallen asleep again.

Next time I awoke, I felt very different. There was no more muddy thinking, no more confusion. It was time to give Clancy the old heave, and get Preston back out on the street. I looked around for Nurse Rogers, and as if she were psychic, she came suddenly through the door. When she saw me turn my head, she smiled.

"You're looking much better," she greeted, "How do you feel?"

"Pretty good," I confirmed, half sitting up, and resting on my elbows. "Tell me, where exactly am I?"

"Monkton General," she replied. "Do you remember what happened?"

"Not too clearly," I admitted. "Some kind of explosion?"

"A car bomb," she replied importantly. "Two people died. You were just far enough to be caught by the blast, and it threw you against the fence. As it happened, it was only a light wooden fence or you wouldn't be here at all. You'd be downstairs."

"Downstairs?" I queried.

"In the mortuary," she replied ghoulishly. "Along with the others. Mind you, you would at least be recognisable. Those two were practically decimated."

Nurse Rogers evidently had a certain relish for the morbid details.

"A bomb," I repeated. "Who were they, some kind of gangsters?"

"Oh no," she denied gravely, "One of them was a private investigator, quite well known it seems. Man named Preston. The other was a young woman, probably his date or something. The police want to talk to you about it, when you're well enough."

"Me? Why?"

"You're the only witness they have," she explained. "There's been an officer waiting outside ever since you were brought in. You're quite a celebrity, Mr. Clancy."

I didn't want to be a celebrity, and I certainly didn't want to talk to any policeman.

"I'm not up to it yet, nurse," I told her weakly. "Do you think I might have something to eat?"

"You certainly may," she assured me, clearly pleased. "Nothing too heavy, at the moment. Milk and a sandwich?"

"That would be fine."

The moment the door closed behind her, I swung my legs over the side of the bed and tested them for reliability. At first, I swayed a couple of times, but I quickly got the hang of it. The important thing to establish was that I could move about independently. There was a mirror on the wall, and I got a mild shock when I saw the bandage over one side of my face. Probing with my fingers, I felt no pain, so presumably there were no cuts.

Pulling at the side of the bandage I peered in the mirror, to see blue welts around the left eye. Maybe they'd been afraid for my sight. Whatever the reason, the bandage was an effective bar to anyone recognising me, and I was grateful for that.

Somebody wanted me dead, and officially that was now my position. So be it. I'd been getting close to something, too close, and therefore I had to die. In my new role, I would be able to work under cover for a while, and possibly come up with some answers. I couldn't stay dead for very long, but it might be long enough for me to do what had to be done.

There was a fire escape outside the window, and I was four floors above the ground. So far so good, but I couldn't leave in hospital pyjamas. Crossing my fingers, I opened the locker, and there were my clothes. Grimy and crumpled, but more than adequate for shinning down fire escapes. Everything seemed set for me to take leave of Monkton General, but it would have to wait until Nurse Rogers thought I was asleep again.

I'd barely made it back under the covers when the door opened. She came in with a small tray, eyeing me with some suspicion.

"Mr. Clancy, you're surely not trying to get out of bed?"

"Oh no," I assured her. "This sheet was getting rucked."

"You should have waited for me," she chided, "That's what I'm here for."

Practised hands tweaked at the bedclothes, and I was neat again. I was all eyes for the sandwich, and my stomach was growling with anticipation.

"Try sitting up," she instructed. "I'll punch these pillows behind you."

I made a big deal out of struggling upright, giving it plenty of sighs and grunts, and enjoying the deft attentions of my guardian. Like the song says, she may not be an angel, but she would do until one came along. The sandwich was good, but I didn't think it would be wise to recover too fast. After a couple of bites, I shook my head with regret, and set it down on the plate.

"I'm sorry nurse, it's a fine sandwich,

but I just don't feel . . . "

I left the sentence unfinished and put on a wan expression. She nodded briskly.

"Don't worry about it," she soothed, "You've had a bad experience, and you probably need a little more rest. Drink some of the milk, and I'll settle you down."

I did as I was told at first. Then, when she began to remove the pillows from behind me, I put on a show of resistance.

"No, no," I protested, putting up a weak struggle against her efforts, "I should be talking to the officer."

Game old Clancy, a citizen to the last. Well, Nurse Rogers knew what was best.

"You will talk to nobody," she decided firmly, "Not until you've had more rest. Be sensible, Mr. Clancy. See how easily I can control you? If you were well, I wouldn't be able to hold you down like this."

She had a point there. Nurse Rogers had plenty going for her in the female department, uniform or no uniform. Any resisting there was to be done would normally have been the other way around.

"Can't stand bossy women," I told her feebly.

"Too bad. Are you going to behave, or do I have to give you a shot?"

That was the last thing I wanted. It was time to capitulate.

"Well," I conceded, "Maybe I am a little tired. I guess I could manage an hour or so."

"Of course you could. Look at you. You can scarcely keep you eyes open, as it is. I'll tell the officer he must wait a while longer."

With that she bustled away, closing the door firmly behind her. There was a brief murmur of voices from beyond the door, then silence. Easing my way out of the covers, I paddled quietly to the locker, and began to get dressed. There were dirt marks on the suit, and I was in need of a shave. What with all that, plus the bandage, my appearance wouldn't have inspired anyone to buy insurance from me. At the same time I wasn't quite villainous enough to arouse suspicion.

I remembered to check the pockets, and they were empty. My freedom wasn't going to be much use to me, unless I could get my hands on some money. That involved getting into the apartment at Parkside, which in turn involved the key. A fine state of affairs when a man can't get blown up by a bomb without having his pockets picked by trusted hospital staff. Then I realised my mind wasn't yet at full stretch. Of course they would empty my pockets, and of course they would put the stuff somewhere safe. Keeping my fingers crossed, I went to the small bedside table, sliding open the top drawer. Inside was a blue plastic bag, which I hefted out and placed on the bed.

It was the first time I'd had any identification with the old-timers, when they suddenly struck gold. No gleaming streak of yellow rock ever looked better than that small heap of belongings. There were the precious keys, plus twenty six dollars and change, not to mention a bonus by way of a crumpled pack of

Old Favorites, and my lighter. I was a man of position again, a man who lived somewhere, and had money in his pocket.

When I got out onto the fire escape, the ground looked a long way down. Despite all my resolve, I hesitated for a moment. One touch of giddiness on the way down, and I would finish the descent in record time. Impatiently, I shrugged the thought away. This was no time for the negative approach. I wasn't going to be given another opportunity to get clean away, and I had better get on with making use of the one I had. Holding tight to the hand rail, and stepping firmly on each tread, I went slowly down.

The ten-minute journey seemed to last for hours, but finally, sweating and limp, I was standing on solid concrete. Pulling myself together, I walked out to the front of the building and hailed a cab. The driver eyed me with some reserve, but cheered up when I told him my destination.

"You don't look too good, mister", he informed me, as we moved away. "What happened? Muggers, I bet."

"Right," I confirmed, lighting a cigarette and relaxing thankfully back.

"Sumpn oughta be done about them people," he pronounced sagely. "Specially in this business. Three times they tried me, you know that? Three times. Didn't do 'em no good though. I carry enough stuff up front here to start my own war. I gotta gun, I got tear gas, a baseball bat with spikes. Oh, I tell you, them people is always sorry when they mess with me. What happened to you?"

He wasn't the type to be fobbed off with a few words. I fed him a long and involved tale, packed with incident, and with a lot of attention to gory detail, and he lapped it up. Finally, we arrived at Parkside Tower and he began to pull in at the front. That I did not want. Once the security staff spotted me, my return to the land of the living would be instantaneous.

"Take me round to the rear, will you? I have to get some things from the car."

At Parkside, the cars of the residents are housed underground. There is a rear elevator, which can only be used with a special key. Once rid of the cab, I made my way between the parked cars, looking at the space where my own should have been. That was one item I'd have to replace at once. Anybody without wheels in my town is practically a vagrant. On the way up in the elevator, I leaned against the side for support, thinking happy thoughts about the bed which was waiting, and wondering whether I dared to take the chance of a couple of hours sleep. When I stepped out into the carpeted corridor, I was taken aback to see a janitor operating a cleaner. Fortunately, he was a stranger, and he merely nodded as I passed. I'd been lucky that time, I reflected, slotting my key into the door of my apartment. Then my luck ran out.

Something hard and familiar jabbed into the base of my spine, and a voice said,

"Inside. Nice and easy."

I've seen all the movies. I know the one about the quick sideways twist of the body, the sharp cutting edge of the hand slicing into vital nerves, the fast knee into whatever it is fast knees go into. I also know that the statistics indicate that the net result is a seven to one chance that the fast knee operator is going to wind up the loser. Given the option, I'll be the one holding the gun every time.

Inside, the new janitor kicked the door shut behind him, and we were alone. Cosy. "Turn around, and drop the coat on the floor," he grated.

He was fifty years old with iron grey hair and a face to match. That told me many things, and in particular to be very careful to follow his instructions. In his work, people don't get into the grey hair category, unless they're good at it.

"You don't dress very neat, do you?" he criticised. "And who worked you over?"

His conversational style added to my worries. Cheap crooks and amateurs are all noisy threats and menace. My new friend was relaxed and calm, just a man doing what he was paid to do. He had no need to show me his muscles. They were there in plain view, in every line of his pallid features. I was alert to the danger, but too exhausted to care much about it.

"Look," I said wearily, "Whatever it is you want, I'm going to have to sit down. It's that or fall down, so if you're going to use that thing, just get on with it."

It wasn't the show of bravery it might have seemed. If the visitor had intended to kill me outright I would already have been well past Nurse Rogers' care. Therefore, he wanted me to talk, and I could do that just as well sitting down. Crossing to the cabinet, I poured myself out a stiff measure of scotch, carted it over to one of the club-chairs and sat gratefully down.

The not-janitor grinned with his mouth, the eyes opting out.

"You got style," he grated. "Who are you and what are you looking for here?"

This was no time for a Mr. Clancy act, and besides, I was too weary.

"I live here," I told him tiredly, "And what I'm looking for is sleep."

"Bullshit," he replied crisply. "Man

named Preston lived here, and he's dead. Try again."

"No he's not," I contradicted. "He's sitting right here. They killed the wrong man. You'll find a brown jacket in the bedroom, with a wallet inside. My sticker is in there, with a nice mug shot. Go see for yourself. And don't look so worried. I don't have a machine-gun under the chair.

He hesitated, then made up his mind. Covering me all the way, he went to the bedroom door and peeked inside. The jacket would be lying on the bed where I dropped it and he'd be able to reach it in two strides. One last look at me, and he decided to take the chance. Then, he stood in front of me, staring at the photograph inside the license, and comparing it with the half-face I was using that day.

"Could be," he muttered, "You don't take a very good likeness, do you?"

"You should see my passport," I replied. "Suppose I tell you what else is in the wallet?"

"Go ahead."

I told him, right down to my precious tickets for the Ella Fitzgerald clambake, due in a few weeks time. He checked each item with great care, but was clearly beginning to believe me. Finally, he put the gun away.

"OK, so you're Preston. This changes a lot of things. I'm going to have to make a phone call. If people are going to believe me, I have to know the whole story, so you'd better tell me exactly what happened."

I told him about the car, and the kids on the bikes, and the way I was caught in the blast. I even told him how I made my exit from the hospital. He listened patiently, and without interrupting.

"You didn't tell me why you went out to the Foxtrot Inn in the first place. Let's hear about that."

My body might have been exhausted, but my mind was still functioning, and the scotch had done wonders. The janitor was clearly a professional, and those people operate within strict limits. He had not been sent to the apartment to harm me, and until somebody told him otherwise, I was comparatively safe.

"Look, I know you're the one with the gun, and I respect that. But I'm no use to you or anybody else once I'm dead. You haven't been told to kill me, and you won't do it unless you're told to. Right now. I'm not going to talk to you or anybody else. I'll tell you what I'm going to do. I'm going to sack out. Make your phone-call, drink my booze, do what you like. I am out of this for one hour, then we'll talk."

Draining the last of my drink, I stood up, waiting for his reaction. He gave me that mirthless grin again.

"You gotta lotta nerve, I'll say that. Any guns in there?" He pointed to the open bedroom door.

"There's a thirty-two in the clothes closet. It's not loaded."

"Yeah, well I'll kind of look after it for you. Are you really gonna sleep?"

"Collapse would be a better word."

He went in first, rummaging around until he located the automatic, which he slipped into a pocket. I pulled off my tie, and crawled onto the bed, shoes and all.

"One hour," he reminded, "Unless my people tell me different."

I didn't think they would, but I didn't much care either. Nurse Rogers had been absolutely right. I really did need more rest.

12

A hand shook at my shoulder, and I opened a jaundiced eye. A face swam at me from the hazy distance, and slowly became the familiar homely mug that belonged to Sam Thompson. He grinned.

"You alive again?"

Forcing myself upright I looked at my watch. It was past four and I'd been unconcious for almost three hours. There seemed to have been some changes.

"What're you doing here?" I queried, "Where's the janitor?"

"You want to talk about janitors?" he replied incredulously, "There's a million things more important, like why aren't you dead, for openers — "

"Not to me," I corrected, "How did you get in here?"

"Florence sent me over with the spare key. Told me to clear out your valuables, so she could lock them up. There was this guy in here, cleaning up, but he went away when I told him who I was. Said to tell you he'd finish later. Now, would you mind explaining a few things?"

He was aggrieved at my absorption with the janitor, and I could scarcely blame him. I told him what had happened, including my recent visitor with the gun, and that seemed to mollify him.

"Well, like they say, all's well that ends well. What're you going to do now?"

"I'm going to get cleaned up," I announced. The long sleep had done wonders for me. "How long've you been here?"

He checked his own watch.

"Lemme see. More'n two and a half hours. Soon as I found you I called Florence. When she finally stopped bawling, she said to let you sleep. I left you till four."

Two and a half hours. So the janitor had had plenty of time to get his instructions. Whatever they had been, they did not include getting rid of me, or my sleep would have been made permanent. I got off the bed, and began pulling off my clothes.

"Make some coffee, will you Sam? And call Florence. Tell her not to spread it around that I'm not dead."

He grunted and went away. I took a shower, ducking my head this way and that, but the bandage got wet just the same. With a thick towel around me, I began to undo it, gingerly at first because I didn't know what I was going to find, then with more confidence. I had the black eye to end all black eyes, but was otherwise undamaged. Dark glasses would cover most of that. Then I shaved off the two-day growth, and was practically a whole man again when Thompson yelled the coffee was ready. When I padded in, he gave a low whistle.

"You ask me, that looks more like a fist than a bomb."

"I hit a fence," I replied haughtily.

"Yeah, you have to watch them fences. Very quick tempered."

I sat down, sipping at the scalding black liquid, and reaching out for the Old Favorites. Somebody had told the janitor to let me finish my sleep, then Thompson had arrived and the gunman had called it quits. For the moment. In one way, that was a pity, because I was anxious to know who had sent him. It couldn't have been the people who planted the bomb. If it had, they'd have told him to finish the job. In fact, the more I thought about it, he would have killed me out of hand, without all that shadow-boxing we'd done. No, they didn't want me, they wanted the something, and the something could only be the missing five hundred dollars. And they didn't want that because it was five hundred dollars, which was not a sum large enough for all this excitement. They wanted it because it was hot, which made it traceable, and put the organisation at peril. In other words, and if it hadn't been for that fence I'd have got there quicker, they were the people who gave Joe Ralph his orders, the Ralfini family of Detroit.

Thompson sat there, frowning at my preoccupation.

"Well?" he demanded, "Are you going to talk to me?"

"There's something missing," I

muttered, "Something here I don't understand."

"Huh," he snorted, "You're talking to a paid-up member, Preston. I don't understand any of it."

I hesitated for a moment. So far, Thompson knew nothing about the money-laundering aspect of the case, and I didn't feel justified in involving him too deeply. On the other hand, I was certainly going to need his back-up in the future, and he had a right to know what he was up against. Mentally, I tossed a coin, but I already knew it had two heads before it hit the ground. I told him the tale.

He listened, with his face impassive as usual. When I was through, he said, "And that's it?"

"That's it."

"So what's your problem? This Ralph killed Mason, not much doubt about that. The mob want their money found. When they get it, maybe they'll kill you, maybe they won't. It won't be nothing personal if they do, just business, that's the way they operate. It all seems quite simple to me."

Either he was dropping the ball, or I wasn't throwing it straight.

"Then who left that bomb in my car?"

"Well they did, natch. Oldest dodge in the business. Those guys have been planting car-bombs since the Model-T."

"I don't buy it," I dismissed, "They wouldn't get rid of me before they got their hands on those bills. No. Somebody else did that, somebody who wants me dead, me, and the money doesn't figure. I call that personal. In fact," and I traced my bad eye with tender fingers, "I call that extremely personal."

"Ah." He let out a long sigh of understanding, "I'm with you now. How about some cherchez on this?"

His pronunciation was so bad, I missed the reference.

"Some what?"

"Cherchez," he repeated, "Cherchez la femme, that's French. How far do you trust this Ellen Ralph?"

"I don't know," I admitted, "I'm not going to say she's not capable of murder, because I never met anybody who wasn't, but I just don't understand why she should want me dead. Don't forget, she's the one who brought me into this in the first place. Why would she do that, and then try to get rid of me the very next day? On top of which, don't forget all her troubles were over by then. The blackmailer was dead, and her old man was locked up. The whole thing was finished, and I certainly hadn't done any harm. Or any good, for that matter."

He wasn't entirly convinced.

"I don't know," he said darkly, "You gotta be able to think like a dame, and I don't think you're any better at it than I am. Very devious people, dames."

I nodded amen to that, but I couldn't come up with one reason why Ellen should want to harm me. Apart from that, the method was against it. Wiring up a car bomb might be lesson one for mob recruits, but it wouldn't come too easily to the singing and dancing star of the That Girl Susie show. She could have had an accomplice, of course, someone a little more in touch with these matters — no. I was making it all too complicated, and

I didn't really believe it was. After all, there were plenty of other people around, who knew about those things. There was the Ralfini family of Detroit, for starters. Then there was the Palm Springs crowd, the people Harry Mason was hiding from. They might be all corporation lawyers and movie stars when they made the front pages, but at root they were the same vicious hoodlums who came out from New York half a century ago. No, I had plenty of real experts to worry about, without fantasising about Ellen Brady.

But I only had one name. Shapiro.

He was the one who tried to get me out of town, and he was the one who told me to get lost. He was the one who could keep me talking long enough to ensure his people had plenty of time to set up the car. It wouldn't be very smart of him, to kill me right outside his own place, but it could be that he was in a hurry. It could be he had to get rid of me before I did something, although I couldn't imagine what. Or — and I liked this better — it could be that he wanted me dead before some other people could talk to me. Yes, the more I thought about it, the better I liked it.

Mr. Shapiro was due another visit.

"Sam, I'm going to need a car. Go and get one, and get back here to me as fast as you can."

He held out his hand. I stared at it.

"Money," he explained, "I'll need money. You know how those people are out there."

Damn. I had no money, and without it I wasn't much better off than I'd been in the hospital room. All my plastic was useless by now. The first thing the banks do in a case of death is to shut off all access to funds. Even if I gave a card to Thompson, and told him the number, he'd find a hand on his shoulder the second he stopped pushing buttons.

Florence Digby.

"Go to Florence," I instructed, "She'll have to use her own money for now. Get all you can. I'm going to need cash before all this is done. You got a gun with you?"

"I won't need it with Florence. That lady trusts me."

It was my turn to hold out a hand.

"Leave it to me, Sam. Get yourself another one while you're out. I don't feel right, sitting around here with just a nail-file."

Without further argument, he pulled a black automatic out from behind him and handed it over.

"Be as quick as I can," he assured me, and left.

I got dressed as soon as he'd gone, and was slipping into my shoes when the buzzer went. Moving softly, I went to the door and peeked through the spyhole. My recent visitor, the not-janitor, stared placidly at the door. I jammed Thompson's gun into the waistband of my pants, behind me. Then I opened up. He stood there, hands in pockets, and inspected me.

"You were right," he acknowledged, "All you needed was sleep."

Then he moved confidently forward, leaving me to close up after him. He wasn't waving any hardware, but then he didn't think it was necessary. We both knew he had it, and that he'd removed mine on his last visit.

"That guy, Thompson, what does he do for you?" he queried.

"Odd things, this and that," I hedged, "He doesn't work for me full-time, he's too lazy."

"I can imagine," he agreed, "Looks kinda dumb to me."

Well, if he wanted to think Thompson was dumb, let him think it. There was no reason why my innocent leg-man should become involved with the people my caller represented, whoever they might be.

"You just missed him, matter of fact," I contributed.

"I know." He turned, to stare into my face, "The guy was up here for more than two hours. What did you talk about?"

That could only mean he'd waited outside until Sam left. Which could only mean he'd been told to stay close.

"Talk?" I scoffed, "It's impossible to talk to that ox for more than five minutes. No, he waited around for me to sleep it off. He still can't believe I'm still alive."

"Hmm. Well, I can't guarantee that's gonna last. There's somebody wants to talk to you. Want me to show you the rod again?"

"Once is enough," I assured him, "O.K. to get my coat?"

"I'll get the coat. The brown one, right?"

I shrugged.

He went into the bedroom, and emerged with the jacket dangling from his fingers.

"I left the wallet inside. Might make you easier to identify. Where did you say Thompson went?"

"I didn't," I contradicted, keeping my front towards him as I struggled into the coat. I left it unbuttoned, partly because of the heat outside, and partly to prevent Thompson's automatic from outlining itself through the cloth, "Matter of fact, he's gone to pick up a car for me."

"Who knows?" he quipped, "Maybe you'll be back for it."

We drove down to Conquest Street, which came as no surprise. Every city has an area which is high on the reformers priority list, and in Monkton the area starts at Conquest. We went into a bowling alley, where the bowling is done at street level, and the action takes place on the upper floors. Upstairs we went into a room where two men sat, watching television.

"Is he in there?" asked the non-janitor.

"Talking to some people," answered the nearest man, "You'd better wait."

I sat down, uninvited, and stared at the screen. When I first came in I thought they were watching newscast of hookers who'd just been picked up by the vice-squad. Now, I found it was the Miss Monkton Beachgirl contest, and I had misjudged the girls very badly. The one being interviewed was in fact a divinity student, whose ambition it was to research the Dead Sea Scrolls. We sat and watched two or three more hopefuls, then a door at the end of the room opened. A man stuck his head around, spotted me and my escort, and jerked his head for us to enter.

I followed my guard into the other

room, where a man sat in a leather-covered chair, watching our approach. He wore a white tropic suit of some silky material and hand-made Italian shoes. The lemon-coloured shirt contrasted with a red knitted tie, and there was a fresh rose in his buttonhole. I've been seeing expensive hoods all my life, and I was seeing one now.

"You're Preston, huh?"

His voice was carefully modulated, as though he'd been to a lot of trouble ironing out the rasps.

"Right," I agreed, "And you?"

He ignored that, waving dismissive fingers at the others in the room.

"Wait outside," he commanded, "I want to have some private talk here. Siddown Preston, take the weight off."

I sat where I could watch both my new host and the door, a move which was not lost on him. He grinned.

"Don't be so nervous. If I wanted anything to happen to you, it would have been done before this. You know who I am?"

I shook my head.

"I don't read the society pages."

Quick flints appeared in his eyes, but he decided to ignore the crack.

"I'm Nick Guardino. I own thirty per cent of Palm Springs. That is, me and my brothers do. Ever heard of a man named Mason? Harry Mason?"

At least we weren't going to be wasting any time dancing around each other.

"Sure," I confirmed instantly, "I met him the other day. He was mixed up in something I was working on. The day after that, he got himself killed. What about him?"

Guardino seemed mildly surprised at the promptness of my reply, and went so far as to incline his head.

"You're talking straight, and that's good. Keep it up, and you could be out of here in no time."

"I can afford to level with you, Guardino," I explained, "You see, I'm not in your business, and I don't even know anybody in Palm Springs. I only have one interest at the moment, and that is to find out who stuck that bomb in my car."

He listened to what I had to say, then cocked his head to one side.

"Suppose you find out. What'll you do?"

"I'll kill him," I said simply.

In saying that, I was taking a chance that my reasoning was sound, and that the man opposite was not responsible for the bomb. If he was surprised by my directness, he gave no sign.

"Suppose it's not a him," he offered softly, "Suppose it's a her?"

It was my turn not to look surprised.

"If it's a woman, then I'll kill her. Don't forget, these are the days of equal opportunities."

"Okay. What did you and Mason talk about?"

"Blackmail, mostly. He wanted twenty five big ones from a woman named Ellen Ralph, otherwise he'd tell her old man she'd been sleeping around. She hired me to stall him until she could raise the money. Her husband found out anyway, and bumped Mason off."

Guardino made a little noise with his mouth, which might have been impatience. Or disbelief.

"Didn't you know who Joe Ralph was?" he queried.

"No, I didn't. I found out since, but I don't see it makes any difference. A husband is still a husband, whatever he does for a living."

My obvious frankness was getting a good reception, and the man from Palm Springs seemed satisfied with the progress we were making.

"Okay," he said again, "I like the way you handle yourself. It's good you should talk straight with me, because I'll tell you this. I got no quarrel with you that I know about, and I don't want one. Now I'll tell you what Mason was really doing here. He worked for me, in a casino. One night he just took off, with over half a million dollars. Makes your twenty five grand sound like car-fare, right?"

I already knew Mason was in trouble with the mob, but I didn't know what kind. Guardino was right, and it had puzzled me. Why would somebody on the run, with half a million in his suitcase, get himself delayed over twenty five measly thousand?

"You lost me," I admitted, "Sounds like somebody played me for a sucker from the beginning. But I don't understand why. There was no need for me to be involved at all. Come to that, why did Mason come here in the first place? Why didn't he just head straight for Mexico?"

"Because he was too smart," came the reply, "Me, I never liked the guy, but you had to give him that. All that South African crap, that's for the birds. A man steals from the Government, an oil company, or the like, sure, he goes to South America. Fifty fifty he gets away with it. But a man steals from us, he's got no place to go, because we got friends. Every place. Mason knew that, and he wouldn't try it."

Which all added up to a very good reason why Mason would not steal from his employers. The only flaw I could find in Guardino's reasoning was that, reason or no, Mason went ahead and did it, just the same.

"Then how come he tried?" I countered.

"He had a friend, is how come. A friend in the organisation. Somebody who would know how to get him fixed up, before he took off. A new identity, passport, all that stuff. A new face, even, it's been done before. While we're wasting our time, and our money, watching all the airports and train stations, Mason is taking life easy right here in Monkton City, and he's got protection. Nice, huh?"

It sounded convincing enough, except for the mysterious partner, who would be setting himself up for mob reprisals.

"I still don't get it," I admitted, "Let's say there was such a man. What's his percentage? He'd have to be in a good place, to have that kind of muscle. Let's say they split the money, took a quarter of a million. What good would it do to him? The minute he started to spend it, you people would know."

The man in the silky suit didn't answer right away. Instead, he took a cigar from a box on the table, rolled it around under his nose, and clipped the end. Then he lifted a gold lighter, and snapped it three or four times without result.

"Gotta match?" he demanded, "Close to three hundred I paid for this thing, and it never works. Guys like that should be arrested."

There was no answer to that. I passed over my own lighter and was relieved when it burst into flames at the first attempt. Guardino puffed away, until his head was wreathed in rich blue smoke, then nodded as though satisfied.

"That's better. You wanta sell this?"

I'd had dealings enough with the mob to understand the patter, and waved a hand.

"A gift," I told him, "My pleasure."

He put the lighter in his pocket, looking pleased.

"Before they did that to your face," he said, pointing, "You were talking with a man named Shapiro. What about?"

My hesitation was only fractional. Nick Guardino might be all sweetness and light at the moment, but that would alter rapidly if I got coy. I told him about seeing Shapiro at Mason's beach hut, and about the offer from Devlin

Associates. The dark eyes were narrow as he followed the tale, and when I was through he grunted.

"I'll give you this, maybe you are some kind of detective, at that. I like the way you put it together. Neat."

"Luck, mostly."

"Nah." He tapped heavy grey ash into a glass tray, "I know smart from luck. What did you make of him, Shapiro?"

I made a face.

"Before I went out there, nothing at all. Since I got this," and I indicated my damaged face, "I've been wondering whether he might have done it. But I can't come up with a motive. I don't know anything that could possibly do him any harm."

Guardino crossed one immaculate leg over the other, and electric blue socks screamed against the sunlight. Electric blue socks?

"You do know something," he contradicted, "You just don't realise you know it. You know that Mason was in touch with that guy, and that's something nobody else would know. With you out of the way, there's nobody to prove the connection. You still ain't figured this, have you?"

"No," I admitted. "I understand what you're telling me, but I don't see Shapiro's profit. I'd say he was pretty well fixed, without asking for this kind of trouble."

"Think about Dallas," he suggested.

I looked back blankly.

"Dallas?"

"Sure. When they knocked off JFK. What happens when somebody kills the president? Who runs things?"

"Why, the Vice-President, naturally."

"Naturally," he agreed, as if I'd said something original, "That's what we got here. Somebody gets rid of Joe Ralph, the number two man moves up. That's how it works."

"And Shapiro is the number two man," I muttered, half to myself, "But, wait a minute, he'd be taking an awful chance. There was no way he could be sure anything would happen to Ralph."

"That's where he was smart," acknowledged the man from Palm Springs, "He took a chance on Joe's temper. Joe doesn't get mad these days, not the way he used to. There was only one thing likely to blow his cool, and that would be his wife cheating on him. Shapiro knew that."

It was all too pat to suit me.

"But, wait a minute," I argued, "This is kind of far-fetched, isn't it? I mean, Joe Ralph must have had a lot of people working for him, hard people. What was to prevent him just sending a couple of soldiers to get rid of Mason?"

For once, I'd contrived to disturb that impassive face.

"Soldiers?" he repeated incredulously, "Where do you think you are, Dodge City? Chicago in the twenties? Nobody puts guns on the streets without the O.K. from upstairs. And when it's personal, like with Ralph and his wife, there's no chance of getting clearance. No chance at all. If Joe Ralph wanted something done, he'd have to do it himself, and Shapiro would know that. Like I say, he figured it all very close. So long as those two guys were shooting at each other, it didn't matter which one went down. Joe Ralph would be finished, either way, and Shapiro takes the job."

It made a grisly kind of sense, particularly listening to Guardino's impersonal delivery.

"And the money, the half million?"

The coarse mouth formed into a pout. "You have to guess about that. Me, if I was Shapiro, I know what I'd do. I'd give the dough back to the Guardino brothers of Palm Springs, with some cockamamie tale about finding it at Mason's joint. That makes Palm Springs happy, and it means we owe Detroit a big one same time, so Detroit is happy. No, you gotta hand it to Mr. Leonard Shapiro, the guy can figure."

In all this chatter, there'd been no mention of the stolen money. Either Guardino knew nothing about it, or he didn't think it was relevant. From his point or view, I could see that it didn't change the reasoning. It so happened that Ellen Ralph had taken some of the bills, thus prompting Ralph to ask questions, but it was really a side issue. If he hadn't learned about the blackmail that way, there were plenty of other ways of tipping him off to what was going on.

Whatever the explanation, I decided to keep my own counsel. Guardino, after all, was from Palm Springs, while the hot money was in the Detroit business. Something warned me it was better kept that way.

"Well, it's been nice talking to you," I said, as though this was some kind of social visit, "Are you through with me now?"

He chuckled.

"They said you had style, and they was right. You ever need a job, give me a call. Don't you want to know how it all comes out?"

I shook my head.

"The less I know the better. I wouldn't want you and your brothers to think I knew too much. I wouldn't want Detroit to think that either. I'm just one man, with a pistol permit, and I don't see myself in opposition to you people."

"Smart, too," he pronounced approvingly, "I like that. Well, I'm going to tell you, anyway. First, and I mean first, there's this half million. I want it back, and Mr. Shapiro, you can believe, is gonna give it to me. Second, Mr. Shapiro has to get dead."

The last thing I wanted was to be party to this kind of information. I held up a hand.

"Don't tell me any more," I begged, "I really don't need this. What you do is your business."

"Correct," he affirmed, "But you're already in this, whether you like it or not. Don't forget, Shapiro already tried to kill you. Your reputation says you ain't the kind to stand for that stuff. An eye for an eye, that's your motto, right? Everybody understands that. The cops, Detroit, everybody. You see what I'm driving at?"

I saw only too well, but I wasn't going to admit it.

"You're going too fast for me," I said without conviction.

Nick Guardino leaned forward, pointing his cigar at me like an accusing finger.

"Then I'll slow it right down, real

slow," he gritted, "First, I get my dough back. Second, you take care of Shapiro."

A voice that sounded distantly like my own said faintly, "Take care of him?"

"Kill him," came the unequivocal reply.

13

At eight o'clock that evening I was fretting around the apartment, trying to figure some way out of the spot I was in. Sam Thompson was parked in front of the tee-vee, with a bottle of scotch and two hundredweight of pretzels beside him. It took an awful lot to worry Thompson, and in any case, he didn't have any problems. He wasn't the one waiting for the phone call, waiting for the message that said the victim was now ready to be slaughtered.

Since I got back from the session with Nick Guardino, I'd studied the situation from every angle, hoping for some brilliant solution to turn up. It wasn't that I entertained any fondness for Shapiro. The guy was too careless with other people's lives to be entitled to any sympathy from me. If the Guardinos were to knock him off, fine. Or the police. If some convenient arresting officer should get into a gun argument and blow off his head, fine.

But it wasn't going to be that way.

Instead, I was elected for the job, and my problem was to find some alternative. There were plenty of people who would consider it no problem at all. The answer was obvious. You went to the police, told them the story, and let them deal with Shapiro. After all, the police are there to protect people, are they not? They would see that no harm came to their informant. If necessary, they would guard a man twenty-four hours around the clock, and the Guardinos could go to hell.

Ha, ha. Ha.

That's what plenty of people would do, but plenty of people don't know the score like I do. From the moment I called the cops, I would be a dead man. Oh, they'd protect me, maybe. For two weeks, a month, even longer, but not for ever. Sooner or later, the guards would be slackened off, finally withdrawn altogether. The city purse just doesn't run to that kind of situation indefinitely. All the Guardinos had to do was wait. One day, the citizens would hear an extra item on the newscast. 'Unknown gunman mows down private investigator', and that would be that.

The only faint hope I had was that things might get out of hand when the Guardinos set about collecting the money Harry Mason stole from them. Maybe Shapiro would put up a fight and start shooting. They would have to shoot back, and that would be the end of it. Fat chance. That kind of thing might happen in a pipe-dream, but not in the big world outside. When those people made their move, the guy would probably be in his shorts, or taking a shower. They'd be quite certain there was no gun handy when they went in for their chat. Then, after they had what they wanted, they would send me in to finish off the job. Very neat. The only person who could provide any lead back to Palm Springs was me, and they knew I'd have to keep my mouth shut. My life was on the line, and I knew the rules. From the point of view of the Guardinos, it was a very neat solution to the problem. It would also suit Detroit. Their number one man, Joe Ralph, had been eased out of the picture by their number two man, and that wasn't something they could ignore. How convenient it was going to be for the Ralfini family, to have their affairs put in order by an outsider, with nothing to point a finger in their direction.

It seemed to me, as I stomped savagely around the room, that I was elected prize chump of the year, with a commission to clean up a lot of dirty linen for two of the country's leading mobs. When it was all over, they could go about their business with no inconvenience, and nobody, not even the police, any the wiser. Except me, and I didn't matter.

And Ellen Ralph, who did.

I was so full of my own problems, I hadn't given a thought to the frightened lady who'd got me into all this in the first place. Now, out of the blue, she came back into the picture with a bang. At the moment, she thought I was dead, but once I came back to life, once I did the job on Shapiro, she would quickly smell a rat. Unless I misjudged her badly, she would try to help me, and she could upset the whole scheme. She was nobody's fool, and once she started telling what she knew, it wouldn't take some smart homicide officer very long to make connections. Somebody like Randall or Rourke, for instance. Show those guys a thread of cotton, and they would soon have a whole shirt, built-in flap pockets et al. Neither the Guardinos nor the Ralfinis were going to take a chance on leaving a thread like Ellen dangling around. She could be in danger right now, for all I knew.

Crossing to the phone, I punched out the number of the place where I'd had my talk with Nick Guardino.

"I can't see the picture," grumbled Thompson.

I ignored him, listening to the burr-burr at the other end. Finally, a voice came on.

"Yeah?"

"Let me talk to Guardino," I said rapidly.

"Who?"

"Nick Guardino. Tell him it's Preston."

"There's no Guardino here, mister. You gotta wrong number."

"Don't hang up," I snapped before he could lay down the receiver, "Tell him this. Tell him it's Preston, and I have to talk with him. And I mean right now."

"You're crazy."

Without waiting for any further discussion, he cut me off. It was no more than I'd expected. Guardino wasn't supposed to be in town and he probably had twenty witnesses to prove he was in Palm Springs at that very moment. Just the same, I thought the message would reach him and that he'd call me back. Thompson tore his gaze away from the tube long enough to look at me curiously.

"What gives?" he demanded, "You gonna resign?"

"Ha, ha. I just remembered about Ellen Ralph. When this is over, she could be a danger to those people, and they're not the kind to take chances."

"So, I want to tell Guardino that if anything happens to her, I will sing. No arguments, no deals, the girl is out of it."

He massaged the side of his face with heavy fingers.

"I don't think you're being very smart," he objected, "You got enough trouble without that. Why go sticking your neck out for some dame?"

Thompson has a great knack for over-simplification.

"Ellen Ralph," I explained patiently, "Is not just some dame, as you put it. Things have got pretty mixed up around here, what with all the excitement — "

"Not to mention your sudden demise," he interrupted.

" — Not to mention my sudden demise," I conceded, "But when you get right back to basics, there's only one that counts. Ellen Ralph is still my client."

"Some client," he grumbled, "You're thousands of dollars out of pocket — "

"Fourteen hundred."

" — whatever. You're out all that green stuff, somebody tried to blow you up, and now you're a bargain basement hit man. I don't see how you owe her a god-damned thing!"

"She's the client," I repeated stubbornly,

"And nobody does her any harm, if I can prevent it."

He didn't argue any more. Instead he leaned forward and switched off the T.V. Then he picked up the cap of the open bottle of scotch and put it firmly back in place.

"I guess the party's over," he said, regretfully, "Something tells me we're gonna get busy suddenly."

I nodded. Some day, when I find enough paper, I'm going to make a list of Thompson's faults. But when it comes to the bottom line, there's nobody I'd swap for him.

Guardino did not call back. I stared at the telephone, willing it to life, but nothing happened. Thirty long minutes came and went, and I realised nothing was going to happen. Not unless I caused it. I picked up the gun which Nick Guardino had thoughtfully returned, and stuck it in my pocket.

"Let's go, Sam," I decided tersely.

"Go where?"

"I have to be sure my client comes to no harm."

Already on his feet, he pointed to the telephone.

"That would be quicker," he pointed out, "Cheaper too."

I looked at him pityingly.

"Did you ever get a call from a dead man?" I asked him, with heavy sarcasm, "She'd probably throw a fit or something."

"And what d'you imagine she'll do when she sees you?" he countered, "Your face looks like somebody just dug it up."

"Simple. You go in first, explain things before she gets a look at me. Now, if you're through arguing, we'll get started."

A lot had happened since that first trip out to Boulder Drive. There had been three cars outside 2024 that time, although Ellen Ralph had been alone in the house, as far as I knew. Now there was only one, the powerful Maserati that looked capable of a vertical take-off. It was coming on dark now, and I parked opposite, peering out at the silent white house.

"Well, what's the pitch?" queried

Thompson, "I go in first, right? What happens then?"

"After you've broken the news to her, about me, I come over and talk to the lady. Don't ask me what I'm going to say, because I don't know. A lot depends on what she's found out since we last talked."

Sighing, to indicate that he had a low opinion of the whole move, Thompson clambered out and slammed the door.

"Gimme two minutes," he suggested.

I didn't have to. He was halfway to the house when there came a deep-throated roar from the Italian engine, and the Maserati hurtled into view, lights ablaze. Moving very quickly for a man of his bulk, Thompson dived into the bushes lining the drive. The car hit the road, made a screaming left, and was gone. I switched on my own motor, and pushed open the passenger door. My shaken companion tottered across to me and practically fell inside. I didn't wait to find out whether he'd broken anything, and he was still struggling to pull the door shut while I made off after the disappearing tail lights.

In any real chase, my standard factory product would have no chance of keeping up with the little red beauty ahead, but conditions were in my favour. We were heading for the built-up area of Glendale, with its speed limits and traffic controls. The driver in front would have no choice but to slow down once we got there. The local shops are very particular about the regulations, and in any case, the layout is against the record-breakers.

"Was it the woman driving?" I demanded, my eyes glued to the disappearing lights.

"I don't know about the woman," he replied, "It was certainly a woman. Why don't you ask me how the broken arm is feeling?"

"You have a broken arm?"

"Not exactly. Just bruised, but it's nice you should worry about me. What do you suppose got into your girlfriend?"

"I don't know, Sam, but it has to be something to do with our business. Either she's scared out of her wits or as mad as hell and we had better find out why.'

I was already touching eighty and

losing my quarry, as we rounded the great swinging bend outside the city limits, when the extra red among all her tail-lights announced that the brakes were being applied. She made a sharp left, and I caught up a valuable few hundred yards. The houses were thicker now, and the occasional stop light came to my assistance. I was no more than a quarter-mile behind when she turned to the right.

And disappeared.

I turned into the road, confident that she would be in plain view, and found myself staring along a wide empty surface. Thompson nudged my shoulder, pointing. Lights glowed briefly against the side of a house along to our left, then were switched off. I drove slowly along, killing my own lights at the same time. The Maserati was tucked in behind some trees, and it would seem Ellen Ralph had gone calling.

"My turn to go first," I announced, "This could be some social call, and we don't want to go upsetting the neighbours. I'll just poke around, see what's going on. If I'm not back in a couple of minutes, you'd better come and check me out."

"Social call," he sniffed, lifting out a wicked-looking snub-nosed revolver, and resting it on his lap.

I went very silently up the driveway. There were lights on at the rear of the house, and if the occupants had any sense they would be outdoors, hoping for an evening breeze to relieve the oppressive heat of the day. A small iron gate stood open, which was an encouragement. If Ellen Ralph was walking the same way she'd been driving, she was in no mood for closing gates. Voices began to filter towards me, as I hugged the shade at the side of the house, a woman, then a man.

" — Explaining to do," and I recognised Ellen Ralph's tones.

"I don't know what you're talking about. You come bursting into my private house — "

Unless I was mistaken, the last time I'd heard the man speak, he'd been warning me to stay away from the Foxtrot

Inn. The lady was calling on Leonard Shapiro.

"Don't get hoity-toity with me, I'm in no mood for it," snapped Ellen.

I poked my head around a trellis fence. Shapiro looked ridiculous in a pair of startling Bermuda shorts, and nothing else. He had obviously just risen from the canvas chair behind him, and was staring nervously at the angry woman who had just disturbed the peace of the evening.

Ellen Ralph had her back to me, feet planted wide apart in an aggressive stance. Shapiro had the advantage of me, because he could see the expression on her face, and he didn't like what he was seeing.

"I'm sure we can straighten this out," he said cajolingly, "Why don't you come and sit down, and we can talk this through like reasonable people."

He made to get a chair for her, but her next words stopped him.

"Reasonable people?" she jeered, "I am not reasonable people, I am mad. Real mad. The only reason I came to you, instead of going straight to the police, is because I might be able to help Joe better, if I know what this is all about."

"Naturally," he soothed, "I'll be only too pleased to help you if I can, but you'll really have to calm down, and tell me exactly what's bothering you."

"Right," she agreed tersely, "I just had a telephone call from some lawyer. He said all Joe's business affairs would in future be handled by you. I was to give you free access to all his papers, and cooperate with you all around. He also said that Joe would confirm what he was saying."

Shapiro put on an expression of understanding sympathy.

"Oh, is that it? Well, dear lady, that's just business. Joe will certainly tell you the same. I'm sure it's something of a surprise to you, but it's really nothing to get upset about."

Ellen walked over to a trolley where there were some bottles, and poured herself a stiff measure of something. Shapiro watched her narrowly, but made no demur.

"Just business eh?" she scoffed, "In the years I've been married to Joe, I've met you about four times, all social occasions. He never mentioned to me anything about doing business with you. Now, out of the blue, you seem to be very big in my life. Just like that. At first, I didn't find it too odd. Joe's always kept his business matters to himself. But then I got thinking about the last few days, and I started doing sums."

"Sums?" he asked, puzzled.

"Sums," she repeated, "Two and two is four. Four and four is eight. The inchworm syndrome, Shapiro."

Her voice was calmer now, but somehow more unnerving than it had been before. The man in the crazy shorts didn't like the change either.

"I'm not following you at all," he said, nervously.

"Try this. I needed somewhere for Harry Mason to stay for a few days. The only real estate person I know is you; so I asked you to help me, fool that I was."

"So? I helped you, didn't I?"

"Right," she agreed, "That must have handed you a laugh, you being Joe's business partner all along and me not knowing it."

"If you're suggesting I told Joe anything about Mason, you're wrong," he asserted, "Go ahead and ask him. He has no reason to cover for me."

"Doesn't he? Well, no matter. The next thing that happened was Joe killed Mason — "

"You're surely not blaming me for that?" he cut in, "Look at yourself, Lady. You're the one that does the sleeping around. Joe only did what any man would do."

I could see Ellen's face clearly now and she flushed as the jibe went home.

"But that wasn't the end of it," she bored on, ignoring what he'd just said, "I hired Mr. Preston to help me, and suddenly he was dead too."

Behind the privacy of the trellis work, Mr. Preston glowed with self-satisfaction.

"A dreadful thing," conceded Shapiro, "But just a coincidence."

"I thought it was odd," she continued,

"That he should have been talking to you five minutes before he was killed. Odd, but no more than that. Then, tonight, when this greaseball lawyer came on the phone, and your name cropped up again, the whole thing fell into place. I don't know how but you set this whole thing up, Shapiro. You used us, all of us, because you wanted to take over Joe's business. Harry Mason is dead; Preston is dead and Joe is locked up. You did all that."

There was silence on the flagged terrace while Shapiro and the woman stared each other out. Finally he gave a helpless shrug.

"Crazy talk," he dismissed, "It makes no rhyme or reason. You don't have a single shred of proof. You're just jumping from one conclusion to another and making a mountain out of it all. Why don't you go home and sleep on it? Tomorrow, if you still feel the same, go to a lawyer. Any lawyer. They'll tell you your story is shot full of holes; it'll never stand up in court."

She set down the glass and began to

fiddle with the sling bag around her shoulder.

"In a court room? No I'm sure you're right. But we don't have a court room situation. We just have us. There's a feature here that doesn't have any standing in the legal system. We call it woman's intuition. You see, I know I'm right, and I'm not interested in the details. My husband is locked up on a murder rap. You may not have pulled the trigger but you're responsible all the same. And Mr. Preston is dead. He did you no harm at all but maybe he stumbled across the truth. I don't know. It doesn't seem to matter right now."

She had the bag open and her hand was inside. Shapiro gave a sneering laugh.

"You're very concerned about Joe, all of a sudden, ain't you? Pity you didn't think about him a bit more while you were whoring around Palm Springs."

When she replied, her voice was matter of fact, almost casual.

"You don't understand at all, do you? Joe Ralph is my husband. There's no-one to look out for him now, only me. That's my job and I'll do it."

The hand that came out of the bag was holding a small nickel-plated automatic. Suddenly, Shapiro's confidence cozed away.

"You're hysterical," he stuttered, "Listen, you don't understand what you're fooling with here. This is family business. Understand what I'm saying? The family is everything — "

"Family business?" she repeated, and her voice sounded far off, "Yes, you're right. My family. Joe's and mine. Now there's only me to look out for the both of us."

The little gun coughed twice, three times. Black holes appeared on Shapiro's chest. He clawed frantically at them, trying to pluck them away as they turned red with his death blood. All the while, he was sinking slowly to his knees, his face a study in pain and disbelief.

I'd already begun to move towards Ellen Ralph as she brought the gun level but there was no way I could have prevented what happened. Now she swung towards me, her eyes blank with shock then widening in disbelief as she saw who it was.

"Mr. — Preston?"

Her tone was still rising as she fell forward into my arms.

14

It took the police eight minutes from the time I placed the call. I could hear car doors slamming at the front of the house, as I sat contemplating the mortal remains of L. Shapiro. He'd never been pretty when he was alive, but in death his naked fatness was obscene.

Ellen Ralph and Thompson were long gone. She had emerged from her dizzy spell in something like a trance, and I wanted her out of it.

"You ever drive a Maserati?" I asked Sam.

"Not till now," he grunted, "What do I do with the lady?"

"Take her home, and keep her there. She talks to nobody. I'll catch up with you later. Oh, and lose the gun. Let's just keep our fingers crossed it doesn't have a story."

I have a great respect for the forensic people, and their system of records. He scooped up the weapon and pushed it into a pocket. Then he led Ellen away. She turned and looked at me."

"It's all right, Ellen. Leave this to me. Go with Mr. Thompson and do exactly as he tells you. I'll be in touch."

Ellen Ralph had no right to kill Shapiro, but then, as I see it, nobody has any right to kill anybody. Yet they do it all the time. The man was dead, and that was that. He'd been going to die in any case, one way or the other, and Ellen had beaten the clock. Now, I had to figure out how to make use of this development, to fit in with what was best for me.

And, as so often, the simple way was best. The upright citizen procedure was needed here, and I've used it many times before, when it suited my book. The police were old young men with bright suspicious eyes and a tough line of questioning. They weren't accustomed to gunshot killings in quiet residential areas, and private investigators reporting in as though a lost dog had been traced. They didn't like me too well, nor what I did for a crust. They liked even less the fact that I told them I was carrying a gun, and were itching for the chance to blow my head off when I handed it over.

My arrest was inevitable. When you have a corpse full of bullet holes and a man nearby with a gun in his pocket, it's a natural assumption that there might be some connection. I didn't know anyone personally at Glendale Homicide, and I wasn't exactly popular when I told my story.

"You admit that you went out there to quarrel with Mr. Shapiro?"

My inquisitor had been a detective sergeant too long, and was clearly disillusioned with his promotion prospects.

"I did," I confirmed cheerfully, "I think it was him who tried to kill me the other night, and I wanted to know why. When I got there, somebody had already killed him, so I called you people."

"With a gun in your pocket," he iterated nastily.

"I have a licence for it, and it hasn't been fired. Your ballistics will confirm that."

"Maybe. Anyway, there's nothing to say you didn't have two guns. You could have used one, and thrown the other one away."

"If I did that, you'll find it. Come on sergeant, you don't have a thing on me. You already tested my hands, and you know I haven't fired so much as a catapult."

He cheered up a little when he talked to Gil Randall on the telephone.

"Zasso?" he echoed, "Zasso? Well, I wonder who this joker is I got in the room here." Clapping one hand over the mouthpiece, he treated me to a slit smile, "This Preston you claim to be, he's dead. Got taken out by a car bomb the other night."

"Let me talk to Randall," I begged him, "I can clear all this up in no time."

Which proved to be optimistic. To Randall I was dead, and he wasn't going to recussitate me on the strength of one telephone call. Least of all when a neighbouring force was questioning me in a murder case. Even if I was Preston, he added sourly, I deserved to suffer a little on account of the inconvenience I caused everybody.

So I spent the night in jail, or what was left of the night when homicide finally got tired of listening to my story. Next day, Murray Klein arrived with a writ and got me out on bail. By that time, the weight of forensic evidence against my being the killer was too strong even for my frustrated sergeant friend. Back home, there was a small knot of media people, anxious to publicise my return from the dead.

Ellen Ralph was being treated by her own doctor for delayed shock, which everybody attributed to the Mason murder, and went out of town to convalesce. I half-expected to get some kind of message from Nick Guardino, but he'd gone home to Palm Springs, and I never saw him again.

The whole messy business was over a month old when I had a visit from an out-of-town lawyer named Benjamin Franklin.

I stared at the card and looked up into

Florence Digby's eyes, which were devoid of expression.

"Ben Franklin?" I queried, "Of the firm of Franklin, Lincoln and Washington, no doubt?"

"That's what it says," she returned frostily, "And I suggest you don't keep him waiting. Mr. Franklin is not the type who normally makes calls on people."

In other words, it was an honour for somebody like me to have somebody like Franklin pay a visit. I waved a hand.

"Usher the gentleman in, Miss Digby."

I usually stand up for visitors, but I don't usually stand to attention. Mr. Benjamin Franklin was everything his name implied. He was sixty-ish, beginning to bow a little, with a mane of silver-white hair. Dressed like a character from Dickens, not forgetting the starched wing-tip collar and the heavy gold watch chain.

"How do you do, Mr. Franklin," I managed, "Won't you have a chair?"

"Very kind," he muttered, absent-mindedly, "Very kind."

Having settled himself down on the

opposite side of the desk, he pressed his fingertips together beneath his chin, and beamed at me, for all the world like Edmund Gwenn playing Santa Claus.

"Well sir, here we are. I hear very good things of you, Mr. Preston. Oh yes, very good things indeed."

It's always encouraging when the clients come with recommendations. This was going to be the one about the missing will, or the long-lost heir to the Van Something millions. Mr. Franklin wasn't one to leave his file-cabinets without good reason, and he'd be anxious to get back to them. I gave him a small prod.

"Good of you to say so." I let him take a look at my expensive cappings. He didn't hold the copyright on beaming, "What exactly can I do for you, sir?"

"Ah!" Thin fingers fluttered, and the silver hair threatened to form a halo, as he shook his head, "Well sir, as to that, nothing further, I assure you. It's already been done. And with complete satisfaction. I represent certain business interests, indeed I may say certain considerable business interests, and you would appear to have rendered them a great service."

The only business people I'd had any remote connection with lately had been the Guardinos of Palm Springs, in the person of Nick, and the Ralfinis of Detroit, in the deceased person of Leo Shapiro. Even their business wasn't my business, because I was working for Ellen Ralph, and she wasn't even a family member. He couldn't mean those people.

"I don't get it, Mr. Franklin."

He nodded happily.

"Then I must explain. There have been — um — events, yes events, which could have brought embarassment to a number of interested persons. There must have been a number of occasions when you could have made life more comfortable for yourself, by the simple process of telling the police exactly what you knew. You elected to keep your own counsel, sir, and there are those who are grateful to you. That is why I am here."

It was hard to accept that this genuine reproduction Uncle Sam was fronting for the mob. They were supposed to have sharp-faced flint-hearted big city lawyers in five hundred dollar suits. This guy looked as if he hung out his shingle on Main Street, Oatsville. And yet, there was no doubting his authority. It flowed from every archaic gesture. Well, at least I didn't have to be so humble with him, now that I knew.

"So you're here. What do you want?"

There was just a small cloud of regret behind his eyes, as he noted the change in my attitude.

"There is the question of your fee," he returned, "Plus certain expenses."

At least he picked a safe area, one in which I wasn't about to start an argument.

"I'm out fourteen hundred, plus bits and pieces," I told him.

Like some ham actor, he produced a thick manilla envelope from inside his coat, and handed it over. Opening it, I counted six thousand four hundred dollars, mostly in big coarse notes.

"It's too much," I told him.

"Pshaw." He really said that. He said 'pshaw'.

I tapped on the table with the envelope, thinking. The only person I was concerned about in the whole mess, was Ellen.

"What'll happen now? To Ellen Ralph and Joe?"

"Happen? Why, nothing. Your prompt action in getting that lady away from all this unpleasantness had been much admired. She will be looked after, until her husband is able to join her again. Which, incidentally, should not be too long. I understand he will have the very best representation."

"I can imagine," I said drily, "If he makes the stand."

For the briefest moment, his eyes held mine, and I felt the naked power in the man.

"My dear sir," he remonstrated, "These are the nineties, not the twenties. Mr. Ralph has been indiscrete, and he had no business to allow his personal feelings to run away with him like that. He will be found something quieter, less responsible. A gaming-house, a talent agency, I really couldn't be precise at this stage."

"O.K. What about the money? There were some people from Palm Springs seemed to think there was some of their property around here."

"You hadn't heard?" he looked faintly puzzled, but shrugged it off. "You know, this business of silence can be overdone, in my view. I see no harm in your knowing that the money was recovered. Recovered and restored to its rightful owners. So you see, there is satisfaction all round. Just one detail bothers me. I know the police searched high and low, and they are not fools, but they could not find that gun. How did you get rid of it, Mr. Preston?"

And that told me something I needed to know. They still hadn't latched on to the fact that Ellen Ralph had killed Shapiro. Let it stay that way.

I smiled knowingly.

"Mr. Franklin, I may need to use that little trick again one day. It would be foolish of me to share it."

He wasn't overjoyed, but he wasn't going to make an issue of it.

"Very well." Mr. Franklin got grandly

to his feet, and I followed suit, "You are satisfied with the arrangements?"

He pointed down at the desk, where those fat thousand dollar notes peeped coyly from the open envelope. I nodded.

"Let's be clear about it. This evens me out. One job, one payment, kaput. I wouldn't want your important people to think this is any kind of retainer. I don't think we'd get along, in any permanent arrangement."

He didn't reply at once, but regarded me levelly, and there was nothing old-world on his face now.

"In my other pocket," he announced, "There is a second envelope. It contains twenty thousand dollars. It was left that I might assess you during this interview and, if I thought you would make a suitable addition to the company, I would pay you the money as a first instalment."

"I didn't get the grades?"

"The envelope is still in my pocket," he pointed out, "There is too much of the individual in you, Mr. Preston. I don't think you're really company material. I bid you good day, sir."

He swept out then, incongruous in his dark clothes, and as unlikely a representative of the hidden economy as I'd never encountered. It wasn't until later that I realised I'd forgotten one of the cardinal principles of the trade.

The ones in black are the bad guys.

THE END

Other titles in the Linford Mystery Library:

A GENTEEL LITTLE MURDER
Philip Daniels

Gilbert had a long-cherished plan to murder his wife. When the polished Edward entered the scene Gilbert's attitude was suddenly changed.

DEATH AT THE WEDDING
Madelaine Duke

Dr. Norah North's search for a killer takes her from a wedding to a private hospital.

MURDER FIRST CLASS
Ron Ellis

Will Detective Chief Inspector Glass find the Post Office robbers before the Executioner gets to them?

A FOOT IN THE GRAVE
Bruce Marshall

About to be imprisoned and tortured in Buenos Aires, John Smith escapes, only to become involved in an aeroplane hijacking.

DEAD TROUBLE
Martin Carroll

Trespassing brought Jennifer Denning more than she bargained for. She was totally unprepared for the violence which was to lie in her path.

HOURS TO KILL
Ursula Curtiss

Margaret went to New Mexico to look after her sick sister's rented house and felt a sharp edge of fear when the absent landlady arrived.

THE DEATH OF ABBE DIDIER
Richard Grayson

Inspector Gautier of the Sûreté investigates three crimes which are strangely connected.

NIGHTMARE TIME
Hugh Pentecost

Have the missing major and his wife met with foul play somewhere in the Beaumont Hotel, or is their disappearance a carefully planned step in an act of treason?

BLOOD WILL OUT
Margaret Carr

Why was the manor house so oddly familiar to Elinor Howard? Who would have guessed that a Sunday School outing could lead to murder?

THE DRACULA MURDERS
Philip Daniels

The Horror Ball was interrupted by a spectral figure who warned the merrymakers they were tampering with the unknown.

THE LADIES OF LAMBTON GREEN
Liza Shepherd

Why did murdered Robin Colquhoun's picture pose such a threat to the ladies of Lambton Green?

CARNABY AND THE GAOLBREAKERS
Peter N. Walker

Detective Sergeant James Aloysius Carnaby-King is sent to prison as bait. When he joins in an escape he is thrown headfirst into a vicious murder hunt.

MUD IN HIS EYE
Gerald Hammond

The harbourmaster's body is found mangled beneath Major Smyle's yacht. What is the sinister significance of the illicit oysters?

THE SCAVENGERS
Bill Knox

Among the masses of struggling fish in the *Tecta*'s nets was a larger, darker, ominously motionless form . . . the body of a skin diver.

DEATH IN ARCADY
Stella Phillips

Detective Inspector Matthew Furnival works unofficially with the local police when a brutal murder takes place in a caravan camp.

STORM CENTRE
Douglas Clark

Detective Chief Superintendent Masters, temporarily lecturing in a police staff college, finds there's more to the job than a few weeks relaxation in a rural setting.

THE MANUSCRIPT MURDERS
Roy Harley Lewis

Antiquarian bookseller Matthew Coll, acquires a rare 16th century manuscript. But when the Dutch professor who had discovered the journal is murdered, Coll begins to doubt its authenticity.

SHARENDEL
Margaret Carr

Ruth didn't want all that money. And she didn't want Aunt Cass to die. But at Sharendel things looked different. She began to wonder if she had a split personality.

MURDER TO BURN
Laurie Mantell

Sergeants Steven Arrow and Lance Brendon, of the New Zealand police force, come upon a woman's body in the water. When the dead woman is identified they begin to realise that they are investigating a complex fraud.

YOU CAN HELP ME
Maisie Birmingham

Whilst running the Citizens' Advice Bureau, Kate Weatherley is attacked with no apparent motive. Then the body of one of her clients is found in her room.

DAGGERS DRAWN
Margaret Carr

Stacey Manston was the kind of girl who could take most things in her stride, but three murders were something different . . .

THE MONTMARTRE MURDERS
Richard Grayson

Inspector Gautier of Sûreté investigates the disappearance of artist Théo, the heir to a fortune.

GRIZZLY TRAIL
Gwen Moffat

Miss Pink, alone in the Rockies, helps in a search for missing hikers, solves two cruel murders and has the most terrifying experience of her life when she meets a grizzly bear!

BLINDMAN'S BLUFF
Margaret Carr

Kate Deverill had considered suicide. It was one way out — and preferable to being murdered.

BEGOTTEN MURDER
Martin Carroll

When Susan Phillips joined her aunt on a voyage of 12,000 miles from her home in Melbourne, she little knew their arrival would germinate the seeds of murder planted long ago.

WHO'S THE TARGET?
Margaret Carr

Three people whom Abby could identify as her parents' murderers wanted her dead, but she decided that maybe Jason could have been the target.

THE LOOSE SCREW
Gerald Hammond

After a motor smash, Beau Pepys and his cousin Jacqueline, her fiancé and dotty mother, suspect that someone had prearranged the death of their friend. But who, and why?

CASE WITH THREE HUSBANDS
Margaret Erskine

Was it a ghost of one of Rose Bonner's late husbands that gave her old Aunt Agatha such a terrible shock and then murdered her in her bed?

THE END OF THE RUNNING
Alan Evans

Lang continued to push the men and children on and on. Behind them were the men who were hunting them down, waiting for the first signs of exhaustion before they pounced.

CARNABY AND THE HIJACKERS
Peter N. Walker

When Commander Pigeon assigns Detective Sergeant Carnaby-King to prevent a raid on a bullion-carrying passenger train, he knows that there are traitors in high positions.

TREAD WARILY AT MIDNIGHT
Margaret Carr

If Joanna Morse hadn't been so hasty she wouldn't have been involved in the accident.

TOO BEAUTIFUL TO DIE
Martin Carroll

There was a grave in the churchyard to prove Elizabeth Weston was dead. Alive, she presented a problem. Dead, she could be forgotten. Then, in the eighth year of her death she came back. She was beautiful, but she had to die.

IN COLD PURSUIT
Ursula Curtiss

In Mexico, Mary and her cousin Jenny each encounter strange men, but neither of them realises that one of these men is obsessed with revenge and murder. But which one?

LITTLE DROPS OF BLOOD
Bill Knox

It might have been just another unfortunate road accident but a few little drops of blood pointed to murder.

GOSSIP TO THE GRAVE
Jonathan Burke

Jenny Clark invented Simon Sherborne because her daily gossip column was getting dull. Then Simon appeared at a party — in the flesh! And Jenny finds herself involved in murder.

HARRIET FAREWELL
Margaret Erskine

Wealthy Theodore Buckler had planned a magnificent Guy Fawkes Day celebration. He hadn't planned on murder.

SANCTUARY ISLE
Bill Knox

Chief Detective Inspector Colin Thane and Detective Inspector Phil Moss are sent to a bird sanctuary off the coast of Argyll to investigate the murder of the warden.

THE SNOW ON THE BEN
Ian Stuart

Although on holiday in the Highlands, Chief Inspector Hamish MacLeod begins an investigation when a pistol shot shatters the quiet of his solitary morning walk.

HARD CONTRACT
Basil Copper

Private detective Mike Farraday is hired to obtain settlement of a debt from Minsky. But Minsky is killed before Mike can get to him. A spate of murders follows.

VICIOUS CIRCLE
Alan Evans

Crawford finds himself on the run and hunted in a strange land, wanting only to find his son but prepared to pay any cost.

DEATH ON A QUIET BEACH
Simon Challis

For Thurston, the blonde on the beach was routine. Within hours he had another body to deal with, and suddenly it wasn't routine any more.

DEATH IN THE SCILLIES
Howard Charles Davis

What had happened to the yachtsman whose boat had drifted on to the Seven Sisters Reef? Who is recruiting a bodyguard for a millionaire and why should bodyguards be needed in the Scillies.